WAITING FOR WINTER LOVE

Amish Love Through the Seasons Book 4

Sylvia Price
Editor: Tandy O, Eagle Eye
Editing & Proofreading

Penn and Ink Writing, LLC

STAY UP-TO-DATE WITH SYLVIA PRICE

Subscribe to Sylvia's newsletter at newsletter.sylviaprice.com to get to know Sylvia and her family. It's also a great way to stay in the loop about new releases, freebies, promos, and more.

As a thank-you, you will receive a FREE exclusive short story that isn't available for purchase.

PRAISE FOR SYLVIA PRICE'S BOOKS

"Author Sylvia Price wrote a storyline that enthralled me. The characters are unique in their own way, which made it more interesting. I highly recommend reading this book. I'll be reading more of Author Sylvia Price's books."

"You can see the love of the main characters and the love that the author has for the main characters and her writing. This book is so wonderful. I cannot wait to read more from this beautiful writer."

"The storyline caught my attention from the very beginning and kept me interested throughout the entire book. I loved the chemistry between the characters."

"A wonderful, sweet and clean story with strong characters. Now I just need to know what happens next!"

"First time reading this author, and I'm very impressed! I love feeling the godliness of this story."

"This was a wonderful story that reminded me of a glorious God we have."

"I encourage all to read this uplifting story of faith and friendship."

"I love Sylvia's books because they are filled with love and faith."

OTHER BOOKS BY SYLVIA PRICE

Seeds of Spring Love (Amish Love Through the Seasons Book 1) –
http://getbook.at/seedsofspring
Sprouts of Summer Love (Amish Love Through the Seasons Book 2) –
http://getbook.at/sproutsofsummer
*Fruits of Fall Love (Amish Love Through the Seasons
Book 3)* – http://getbook.at/fruitsoffall
Waiting for Winter Love (Amish Love Through the Seasons Book 4)
– http://getbook.at/waitingforwinter

The Christmas Arrival – http://getbook.at/christmasarrival

Jonah's Redemption: Book 1 – FREE
Jonah's Redemption: Book 2 – http://getbook.at/jonah2
Jonah's Redemption: Book 3 – http://getbook.at/jonah3
Jonah's Redemption: Book 4 – http://getbook.at/jonah4
Jonah's Redemption: Book 5 – http://getbook.at/jonah5
Jonah's Redemption: Boxed Set – http://getbook.at/jonahset

Songbird Cottage Beginnings (Pleasant Bay Prequel) – FREE
The Songbird Cottage (Pleasant Bay Book 1) –
http://getbook.at/songbirdcottage

Return to Songbird Cottage (Pleasant Bay Book 2) – http://getbook.at/returntosongbird

Escape to Songbird Cottage (Pleasant Bay Book 3) – http://getbook.at/escapetosongbird

Secrets of Songbird Cottage (Pleasant Bay Book 4) – http://getbook.at/secretsofsongbird

Seasons at Songbird Cottage (Pleasant Bay Book 5) – http://getbook.at/seasonsatsongbird

The Songbird Cottage Boxed Set (Pleasant Bay Complete Series Collection) – http://getbook.at/songbirdbox

The Crystal Crescent Inn (Sambro Lighthouse Book 1) – http://getbook.at/cci1

CONTENTS

CHAPTER 1: AN UNEXPECTED VISITOR

Mary Lapp sat in the chair by the window. Her needlework lay abandoned in her lap as she stared out of the window into the darkening landscape. The chair that Mary was currently occupying used to be her sister's favorite spot, but since she had left, Mary had adopted it as her own. She could see why Rachel had loved it so. The chair gave the best view of the small front yard with the distant hills visible on the horizon. It was like staring into an oil painting. Mary was alone in the living room except for Muffin, the small black and white kitten who was curled up on the mat in front of the fire. The Lapps had never owned a cat before, but, when Mrs. Lapp had come across a rat's nest in the kitchen, she had insisted on a feline to deal with the pests. Mary knew that the cat's purpose was to get rid of the rats, but she couldn't help feeling that the little thing had already become part of the family.

"Can we give him a name?" Mary had asked.

It was not common practice for Amish to own pets except if they had a purpose, such as catching rats, and neither was it standard practice to name animals.

"If you must," Mrs. Lapp had said, with a wave of the hand.

Her youngest would give it a name with or without her permission.

"Muffin" had come about after Mary found the kitten curiously investigating a batch of friendship muffins that her mother had baked for the new schoolteacher.

"You'd better not eat *Maem's* muffins," Mary had whispered to the kitten.

Now Muffin lay purring contentedly on the floor while Mary gazed out of the window. She sighed. It was hard to imagine that just a little while ago, the hills were a lush green and the trees had spread their shade generously across the ground. Now the leaves had gone, and while it would still be a few weeks before the first snow, the landscape had already experienced two touches of frost, which had left their indelible mark. Mary had strolled through the frozen garden earlier in the day. As she walked, her boots had crushed brown blades of grass, and all the last vestiges of the garden had turned the same color. The birds chirped no longer, for their home was now down south. It was eerie. *Travel safely*, she'd thought.

Mary replayed her garden adventure, smiled to herself, then imagined Aaron's reaction had he caught her looking so melancholic. He would have lectured her to be grateful for the winter because it meant rest for the weary. Also, she ought to look at it as more than just a precursor to the spring, but as something equally important. She could hear his voice telling her how the cooler temperatures and shorter days would give plants the time they needed to rest, to go dormant, and gather up energy for spring. Mary would've listened in two minds. The first, grateful for the new insight, and the second, resentful for knowing it already from her recent experience. Aaron's sagacity was one of his many traits that she already missed. He had a way of seeing the world that was refreshing and different from Mary's perspective. She breathed deeply.

Aaron's announcement regarding his *rumspringa* had come as a surprise to Mary. Though she had recovered from the initial shock, her heart was heavy at the thought of losing him. She had known him all her life; the idea of him being gone seemed strange. Her only relief was that she had finally discovered how she truly felt about Aaron. She had feared losing out on love, but her walk home had given her pause. While she'd miss him terribly, she could live without him. A girl does not need much experience in romance to imagine that the idea of being separate, of not being able to see one another, would be too difficult to bear. That feeling should tear her apart and leave her in pieces. Mary didn't feel torn. She felt sad. She would undoubtedly miss Aaron, but she was happy for him. Thus, their separation would be a bittersweet one, not an unbearable one.

Mary had once lost someone else when she was younger. She had not thought about him in years, yet Aaron's announcement had brought this first departure to the fore. When Mary had been a child of about nine, she'd believed herself to be hopelessly and irrevocably in love. The boy had not been particularly outstanding, nor had he possessed any remarkable talents, and yet Mary had been convinced he was her one true love.

Abe's family had moved to Erie from a community in the East. No one had known much about the family. They'd appeared to be good people. Mrs. Lapp and Mary had taken a basket of baked goods around to their house to welcome them to the community. Mary had worn a blue dress that day. As they had entered the property, Mary had spotted a boy hanging upside down from the branch of a large oak tree. He'd been about twelve, and as they'd walked past, he had grinned at Mary.

"Abe, come inside and meet the Lapps," his mother had called.

A few moments later, Abe had stepped onto the porch and greeted them. Mary had noticed he had a leaf in his hair and a grubby mark on his chin.

"Hello," Abe had said enthusiastically. "I'm Abe."

From that day, Mary and Abe had spent a great deal of their time together. It had seemed as if they'd had everything in common. Then, out of nowhere, Abe had told Mary that his family had decided to move to another community.

"But you've only been here a few months," Mary had cried.

"I know," Abe had agreed, "but my *maem's schweschder* is sick, and she wants to go and care for her."

"But what about us?" Mary had asked.

"I promise I'll write and come back as soon as I am old enough," Abe had promised.

The news had devastated Mary, although she could chuckle about it now. There was a little comfort in Abe's promise to write to her frequently. Abe had kept his promise to Mary, and for weeks after he had left, she had received letters from him in which he detailed his new life and how much he longed to see her. Yet as time went on, Abe's letters had arrived more infrequently and were half-hearted and shallow. The letters had eventually ceased. Mary recalled her anguish in waiting for the letters to arrive, foolishly hoping that it was a mistake at the post office that had caused the delay. The pain had cut deeply. *People can betray me,* she'd concluded, *even if I never betray them.* It had been a tender age to lose her innocence.

Denial is the step in the grieving process most like mud: everyone gets stuck there. It took Mary months to overcome her pain at having lost Abe, to finally accept that he had moved on, and to do the same. Despite these revelations, she secretly held on to the idea that Abe might return for her one day. It was a childish fantasy that now made Mary blush, but it was something onto which she had clung whenever she felt adrift. It had remained Mary's little secret, for fear of mockery. She had been in love, perhaps not in the grown-up sense, but in a way she understood.

While Mary had not thought of Abe for many years, she now wondered if perhaps what had happened with him and the way things had ended had made her afraid of love. Had she been aloof with Aaron? Did she not have the right touch? Was it because of Abe? It was true that no heart is as tender as a young heart. If she had not met Abe and been jaded by the whole saga, perhaps she would be like Abigael and Sarah, with a beau on her arm and marriage on the horizon. *Will my broken heart cause me to be an old maid?* she wondered. Indeed, the very idea of love was something Mary ran from as if it were dangerous. Mary guarded her heart fiercely for fear of being hurt again. Opening herself up to navigate love was, therefore, anathema.

Muffin stretched happily in front of the fire, his tail curled in a question mark.

"You don't have any worries, do you?" Mary said to the contented feline. It lazily opened one eye only to close it again.

Mary looked at the needlework in her lap and rubbed her eyes. She was supposed to be making lined bags stuffed with dried rosemary as Christmas gifts for her mother, sister, and friends, but her heart was not in it. She closed her eyes, ready to drift off when a knock at the front door jerked her out of her fatigue. She sat up. No one had been expected to call. Then there was a second knock. Her family would have let themselves in. *Who could it be?* Mary hurried to the front door lest the icy wind leave the poor visitor stranded on the porch.

"Samuel?" Mary breathed.

Samuel King looked at her, red-nosed and rosy-cheeked from the cold, yet otherwise still his handsome self.

"Hello, Mary." Sam flashed a white smile.

"What are you doing here?" Mary asked.

"How about you invite me in, and I'll tell you."

"Of course! How thoughtless of me." She opened the screen door, and Samuel stepped through. He remembered the place, fondly.

"Are your folks here?"

"My *maem* is out visiting Rachel, but my *daed* is in the study," Mary explained. "Would you like me to call him?"

Samuel shook his head. "I came to see you."

"Me?"

Samuel nodded.

Mary showed him into the living room. She sat back down in her chair, and Samuel sat opposite her. He reached over and tickled the cat gently behind its ears, eliciting a rumbling purr.

"You like that, boy?" Sam murmured to the cat.

"Muffin," Mary supplied.

"No, *danki*. I'm not hungry." Sam smiled and sat back in his chair. "I know that my visit is unexpected. It has been a while since we've seen one another."

Mary grinned. Sam interpreted this to mean that she was remembering him fondly, but Mary hadn't gotten over the

"Muffin" misunderstanding, the conversation having moved along too quickly for her to correct him. They had last spoken in the King barn. Mary had taken the bold step to warn him that his fiancée, Mary's sister, Rachel, was threatening to do the Amish equivalent of eloping: moving away to another community in order to marry another. Her heart had raced, for Samuel was an imposing man, and his father, should he have overheard, would have lost his temper. Not even the severest of summer storms could crackle like old man Levi. It had been the boldest thing she had ever done, but she had gone to Samuel to save their family. How the situation had unfolded was not what she had expected. In the end, Samuel had chosen to leave the community for a time of exploration and independence, a belated *rumspringa*. Mary had not seen him since, though Hannah King had provided updates about her brother from time to time.

"I never really apologized for confronting you in the barn."

"I'm glad you did," Samuel admitted. "You saved both your *schweschder* and me from a lot of future heartache. Our intended marriage was a commitment neither of us wanted."

It was good that Samuel did not hold a grudge. For years, the Lapps had thought that Samuel would become part of their family. He had grown up with Rachel, and Mary had always had a fondness for him. She had wondered about the day in the barn and whether he might think of her as interfering or inconsiderate. It was good to know that he had understood her intentions as she had meant them.

"You still haven't told me why you are here," Mary said.

"I am on winter break," Samuel said. "Home for Christmas."

"Lovely! I am sure your folks are thrilled you are back." She regretted saying it as soon as she had said it.

Samuel tightened his jaw. His relationship with his parents was complicated.

"How is community college?"

"*Gut*," Samuel replied. After a momentary hesitation, he added, "I'm sorry to just come around like this, but I need your help. I think I may be in trouble."

CHAPTER 2: SAMUEL'S STORY

"What kind of trouble?" Mary asked.

Samuel sighed. "It's a long story. Let's just say I'm helping a homeless man."

Mary nodded and shifted slightly in her chair.

"You must understand, Mary, that the *Englisch* world is wildly different from our own. They receive education from an early age and continue until they are in their mid-twenties or even older. Their thirst for knowledge is something that I never understood until I lived among them," explained Samuel.

Mary said nothing.

Samuel continued. "I knew when I left our community that I was in search of something different. Often life here can be so predictable and stagnant. When I started at community college, I could not believe how many resources were available to me—not just books, but technology that could answer every question you've ever had with just the touch of a button."

There was excitement in Samuel's voice coupled with guilt. Surely, it was his Amish upbringing that caused it. *How strange it must be for him to admit to breaking the rules of the Ordnung,* Mary thought.

"The more time I spent studying, the more I felt like there were so many things I didn't yet know. I craved to learn more. One day, I saw a poster for a Bible study group that met twice a week off-campus. I was curious about how the *Englisch* studied religion and so I went along." Samuel paused. Mary anticipated his remorse. Guilt spelled itself out across his face. "I knew that it was wrong, but I told myself that it was only wrong in the context of our community and not in the *Englisch* world."

Most Amish across North America believed in reading solely from the German Bible which Martin Luther had translated. None ever preached from the English translations. Few in Samuel's community owned or read an English Bible. It simply was not done. Martin Luther had translated the Holy Scriptures so that his parishioners could understand God's Word and read it for themselves. This would free them from the influence of Catholic priests reading from the Latin, which the masses did not speak, and then telling them all what the Bible meant. The irony, however, was lost on virtually the entirety of Samuel's community: that the High German translation to which they clung, and which many present-day Amish did not fully understand, was first produced to ensure that all who read it understood it.

"I had my Bible with me, tucked safely under my arm, but I was so curious about how it was read in *Englisch* that I accepted the copy they handed to me."

Mary tried to hide the shock she felt, but she did a poor job.

"I don't blame you if you judge me, Mary. I just hope you can understand that I was living with the *Englisch,* so I felt that I needed to open myself up to their ways."

"Is it much different?" Mary asked curiously.

Samuel nodded. "I could easily understand everything. It got me thinking about the *Amisch* rules, many of which do not exist in the Bible itself. I began to study *Ordnungs* across several communities to understand how the *Amisch* decide which rules to follow."

"And what did you discover?" Mary could hardly contain herself. Her nerves were shot lest her father, the community's bishop, overhear them, yet this new revelation into an unknown world by someone trusted, proved irresistible.

"That many *Ordnungs* consist of rules which are not in the Bible. Instead, they are *Amisch* customs placed under the umbrella of religion despite not being present in the Bible."

Mary sat wide-eyed, unsure of what to believe.

"My time in the *Englisch* world has taught me much, Mary, but one of the greatest lessons I've learned thus far is that the *Englisch* are interesting people from whom we can learn a great deal. This is part of the reason now that I find myself in need of help."

Mary waited.

"Two days ago, I was working on some renovations at a hospital as part of my internship. I went on break to find a man crying, covering his ears, and rocking himself forward and back. I felt compassion for him, so I approached him to offer my help.

Can I help you? I asked. When I looked into his face, something was off.

Shall I call a nurse? I asked.

He grasped my hand tightly and begged, *Just get me out of here.*

"I don't know why I didn't call for help. I think it was because of the look in his eyes. It was as if he were a rabbit caught in a snare. His eyes were wild with terror yet sorrowful. That's the best way that I can explain it."

"So, what did you do with him?" Mary asked.

Samuel hesitated. "He was in a bad way, Mary. I couldn't just leave him."

"What did you do, Sam?" Mary repeated.

"I took him back to my apartment."

Mary was astonished by Samuel's revelation. When he'd knocked on her door half an hour before, she never imagined that he would have such a tale to tell.

"I know it may seem strange, but he needed my help, Mary," Samuel continued. "I gave him a blanket and some water, and he fell asleep almost as soon as he sat down on the couch. I know this story is a strange one, but I do believe that *Gott* wanted me to help him."

"So, what happened?"

"He stayed with me."

"But why did you not seek help?" Mary asked.

"He begged me not to," Samuel said. "He was terrified he'd be sent to a psychiatric hospital. I had to find out what it meant. It's pretty bad. He has nightmares. He screams a lot. It's always the same thing. He hardly has an appetite."

"What does he scream?"

"It's usually, *Hassan*, or *I tried to save you*. He won't explain it to me."

"Why was he so sad?"

"I think the construction noises reminded him of something. He's always on edge, and loud noises startle him far too easily."

Samuel's compassion was evident. Mary admired him for his charity, but she was also concerned by what she heard. This *Eng-*

lischer needed more help than Samuel could offer him.

"Where is he now?" Mary was enthralled, but she could not fathom the trouble Samuel claimed to be in, not from the story thus far.

Samuel exhaled sharply before continuing. "This morning, after a particularly bad night, the landlord came to tell me that there had been noise complaints and reports that another person was living in the building without permission. I knew it would happen eventually, but I'd hoped we would have a bit more time to figure things out. He told me to get him out before the end of the week."

"So, what did you do?"

"What could I do?" Samuel said. "It's the winter break. I would be here for three weeks.

I packed a bag and bought two train tickets. We arrived in Erie yesterday evening."

"You brought him here?" Mary thought she might faint. The Amish were not to mingle with the *Englisch*, especially not at home. It was necessary for business but was forbidden socially.

"What was I supposed to do?"

"Do your parents know?"

"No. We walked to my family's farm. With my folks in bed, I snuck inside to get the key to the Manager's Cottage."

Mary was aghast and a little thrilled. This was a side of Samuel she'd never seen before. There would be severe repercussions should they be caught, yet this new Samuel, more assertive and risk-taking, was…attractive.

"That is why I need your help, Mary. I locked the guy in the cottage, but it is only a temporary solution. I need to find a way to help him before my *daed* finds out that he is there. You know how he is."

Indeed, all knew how he was: a thorn in the side! There was hardly a man more embittered than Levi King. Mary nodded, but she was unsure what she could do to help.

"I know this is a lot to ask of you, but who else could I turn to? You are the most compassionate, courageous, and level-headed person that I know."

"*Danki*," Mary said, but this was serious. "I'm glad you think of me as those things, but I don't know what I can do to help, Sam."

Samuel sighed. "Okay. I should not have brought this problem to you. I'm sorry to have burdened you, Mary. I'll go now." Samuel arose quickly and headed for the door, his disappointment palpable. It made Mary want to help. Something stirred within her.

"Wait!" Mary cried louder than was wise. "I don't know what to do *yet*, but I'll help you the best I can."

Samuel beamed. Mary felt herself grow warm under his gaze.

"I know this is a time-sensitive issue," Mary continued, "but I need time to think. Can you meet me tomorrow at the Weaver farm? There is a plot on the edge of the eastern side where we have a garden. We can talk there without being disturbed."

Samuel nodded. "I know the place. *Danki*, Mary. You have no idea how much I need your help."

Mary lost herself in his gaze. A flush of excitement rose to her cheeks, leaving them beet-red from the exhilaration she felt. There was also something else she could not describe. There was no time to put a word to it, however, for she now felt the burden of responsibility, for this *Englischer's* well-being had fallen on her.

It was a significant load to carry. She showed Samuel to the door, her mind racing to find answers. Rosemary bags and Christmas gifts were the last thing on her mind. Samuel had returned and brought with him a new sensation, at least as far as Mary was concerned.

CHAPTER 3: REFUGE

The following afternoon, Mary took the familiar path towards the garden. Each step forward seemed to birth a new thought or idea in her mind. She was unable to concentrate entirely on one single thing. Since Samuel's visit the day before, Mary had thought of little else other than the condition of the *Englischer* he'd brought home. It seemed to her that he needed professional help, but only someone who wanted help could be helped. A lifeguard cannot save a man who hasn't first given up on trying to save himself.

Mary was running late. She quickly pushed the little gate open. Its hinges creaked their objection as she walked through. Mary looked around and spotted Samuel standing at the other end of the garden, leaning against the fence, contemplating the Weaver acreage that stretched as far as the eye could see. It was one of Mary's favorite spots to think.

"Hello," Mary greeted as she approached.

Samuel turned around and smiled at her. "Mary! I was worried you had changed your mind."

"Do you think I am so contrary?"

Samuel smiled. "Let's just say that I wouldn't blame you for having second thoughts."

Mary nodded. She had agreed to help, and she would keep

her word. However, her promise was moored in a guilty harbor; there would, in all likelihood, be little protection from the storm. "How is he?"

Samuel shook his head and sighed.

"I went to see him this morning before dawn chores and found him asleep on the bathroom floor. I don't know how long he had been there, but he was ice cold. I feel guilty leaving him all alone, but it's difficult to sneak off and see him. I usually tell my folks that I am going on a walk, but they are becoming suspicious about the number of walks I take a day."

Mary nodded. "Is he eating?"

"Some, but not enough."

I can help by bringing him food?" Mary offered, relieved. It was the first clear notion she'd had about how she could help.

Samuel looked relieved. "That would be a great help, actually. My *maem* thinks I've developed a horse's appetite since coming home. The truth is, I've been hiding bits of food in my pocket to give to him."

"I'm sure that I can manage to get some food without anyone noticing. Should I meet you at the Manager's Cottage on the farm?"

Samuel stiffened. "I'm not sure." The truth was that Samuel trusted Mary, but he was not sure how the *Englischer* would react to her.

Mary frowned.

"It's not you, Mary. I just think it might be too soon."

Mary nodded. "I understand. Let's meet here, in the garden, instead?"

"*Ya*," Samuel said. "That would be *gut*."

"Same time tomorrow?" Mary suggested.

Samuel looked at her with doe-like eyes. "He could use it today." He was irresistible.

"Wait here," Mary instructed. She then turned on her heel and left.

When Mary returned, she had a basket of bread, cold meats, and preserves.

"This is a feast," Samuel said in awe. "How on earth did you manage it?"

Mary smiled mysteriously but said nothing.

Samuel took the basket and gazed at Mary in amazement. She had grown up so much in the past couple of years. She was a woman now, confident and kind. He had a new admiration for her, one that he had never felt for her before.

"This should last him a few days," Mary said.

"*Ya*," Samuel agreed. "So, should we meet again at the end of the week?"

Before Mary could answer, the gate creaked open, and in came the Weaver sisters. They were carrying baskets and chatting away, but they stopped talking as soon as they spotted Mary and Samuel.

"Hello," Sarah said in surprise. "We didn't expect to find you here."

Mary smiled. "Hello."

Abigael said nothing, choosing, instead, to eye Mary and Samuel, which intensified her curiosity.

"Samuel King!" she said suddenly. "We didn't know you were back."

Samuel smiled nervously, afraid of what it might look like to be found with his former fiancée's sister in a secluded place. "Just for the winter break."

"Is Mary showing you around the garden?" Sarah asked.

"*Ya*," Mary interjected. "Samuel was curious about what we had been doing this year."

"Why didn't Hannah offer to show you?" Abigael asked mischievously.

Samuel looked stumped.

"She was too busy helping out Mrs. King," Mary explained, keeping her wits about her. "They have family coming to stay for Christmas, and Mrs. King wants the whole house cleaned." Mary was amazed at how quickly the lie came to her.

"Mmm," Abigael mumbled.

"Why are you two out here?" Mary asked. "It must be a rare sight for the garden to see you."

Abigael scowled at Mary's remark, then quickly regained her composure.

"We just came to see if the winter jasmine had buds yet," Sarah explained.

"I walked past there earlier and didn't see any buds," Mary confessed, "but I didn't have a proper look."

Sarah smiled appreciatively. "Well, we might go and have a look anyway," she said. "Come, Abi."

Abigael looked as if she did not want to leave.

"See you around, Mary," Sarah said, pulling her twin towards her.

Mary smiled and waved. Samuel nodded.

Abigael gave them one last look before following her sister towards the winter jasmine growing on the garden's western side. Mary and Samuel waited until they were gone, then spoke in hushed tones.

"Abigael Weaver is still as terrifying as I remember," Samuel remarked.

Mary giggled.

"You don't think they overheard us, do you?"

Mary shook her head. "No, I don't, but we should be more careful in the future. I thought that they had stopped coming to the garden. I guess I was wrong."

Samuel nodded in agreement. There was something romantic about whispering to each other even if the conversation was serious and not the least bit flirtatious. Sam had to get out of there lest he never return to his charge.

"Well, I'd better go," Mary said. "I promised Rachel I'd look after Jo this afternoon so she and Noah could go—" Mary stopped herself as soon as she realized what she was saying. She bowed her head. "I am so sorry. I didn't mean to bring up Rachel and Noah."

Samuel smiled kindly. "That is water under the bridge, Mary," he said, casually. "I'm glad that Rachel and Noah are happy. They deserve it after everything that happened."

Mary smiled and nodded. "I'll see you Thursday."

"See you then," Samuel agreed. He watched as Mary made her way along the garden path and towards the gate. When he'd lived in the city, he had not allowed himself to think about the life he had left behind. He knew that it would do no good, so he had compartmentalized his life. Ever since he had returned to Erie, he had been so preoccupied with the *Englischer* that he had not thought about Rachel nor Noah. Or their history. That compartment's lid, however, was beginning to break its seal.

*　*　*

Mary and Samuel met again as they had arranged and the

Sunday after that. To complicate things, the Weaver sisters had found a renewed interest in the garden. Mary suspected that it had nothing to do with gardening. Mary and Samuel had heard the gate creak and had been forced to retreat. Abigael and Amos arrived. From their hiding place, Mary and Samuel could see Abigael looking around as if she were searching for someone.

"This is unlike you," Amos noted.

"What is?" Abigael asked innocently.

"Wanting to spend the afternoon strolling around the garden."

Abigael had laughed airily and patted Amos on the arm. "Don't be silly, Amos. I love strolling around outdoors."

Amos had raised his eyebrows but said no more.

The next time, Sarah and Jacob had forced Mary and Samuel into hiding. Mary was then convinced that their run-ins were more than just a coincidence.

"What are we doing here?" Jacob asked.

"Abigael said she left her *kapp* in the garden the last time she was here," Sarah explained. "She asked me to come and look for it."

"Well, why didn't she come and look for it herself?"

"Apparently, she did, but she asked me to look, too. She knows *Maem* will be furious if she loses it." Sarah seemed to be looking through the trees to find the lost *kapp* as though it were perched on a branch.

"I thought you said no one comes here anymore," Samuel said.

"They don't," Mary replied. "At least they never used to." She knew very well that Abigael was orchestrating these garden visits in the hopes of running into her and Samuel again. Mary guessed that Abigael kept watch from her bedroom window, which looked onto the garden, and every time she saw them arrive, she made some excuse to come out. She chose not to share it with Samuel for fear it would make him shy to be with her. Mary appreciated the man's attention and was loath to part with it.

A week after Samuel first visited Mary, they again met in the garden. Mary had seen the Weaver sisters on their folks' buggy heading into town that morning. She and Samuel could finally meet without interruption. It was a relief for Mary, for she had something serious to talk about.

"Mary," Samuel said.

"Hello," Mary returned.

Samuel reached for the basket, but Mary stepped back. The man was puzzled.

"I want to meet the *Englischer*," Mary proclaimed.

Samuel stared at her, incredulous.

"Before you say anything, just listen," Mary continued. "It's been a week since you told me your story, and since then, I've been doing my best not to imagine the poor man locked up in that cottage. I've tried to believe that the food I am giving you is enough, but I've realized it isn't. Last night, lying in bed, I decided that it's not fair. I can't just go on imagining. I need to see him for myself." Mary studied Samuel's face closely as she spoke. To her surprise, Samuel smiled.

"You're right, Mary. It isn't fair to you. I didn't want you to meet him because I thought he might react badly, and I didn't want you to be hurt or shocked. But if you want to meet him, then I won't stand in the way."

"*Gut*," Mary said. "Then, let's go."

"Now?"

"*Ya*. Now."

Samuel thought it best not to contend with a determined Lapp, so he did not argue. Mary had always been strong-willed, and if she decided on something, there was very little anyone could say or do that would change her mind. Still, he looked at her pitifully as if to say, *Please, can we do this another time?* There was nothing doing. Mary was unmoved.

"We need to go around the south field because my *daed* and the farmhands finished working there last week. That way, no one will see us."

Mary nodded. She did not need Samuel to show her the way. When they were children, they would spend Saturday afternoons on the King Farm, exploring. While Mary was always the youngest, Rachel and Samuel never treated her so, and they always included her in whatever adventure they had planned. So much so that Mary knew the Kings' property as well as Samuel did.

They walked silently. It was only when they approached the Manager's Cottage, that Mary was torn away from her inner dialogue and into one with her escort. She looked for some indication of life, such as a shadow in the window or smoke coming from the chimney but saw nothing.

"Why is the cottage empty?" Mary asked.

"My *daed's* last farm manager, Mr. Miller, moved out at the beginning of November," Samuel explained.

"And he hasn't found a replacement yet?"

Samuel shook his head. "He's stalling, I believe. I think he is hoping that I'll come home and take over as a manager of the farm."

"Will you?"

Samuel shrugged.

Mary and Samuel approached the cottage and climbed the two steps onto the porch. Samuel reached into his pocket and removed the small key. He inserted it into the lock as he pushed open the door and stepped inside. As soon as they had stepped into the room, Mary heard hurried footsteps and saw a blur racing toward them. She instinctively stepped back as Samuel was thrown against the wall so hard that the cottage shook. Mary was so shocked by the scene. A whimper escaped her lips once she realized her own helplessness. The *Englischer* had Samuel pegged to the wall by his neck. His eyes were wild, his breath ragged, as he pressed his hand around Samuel's throat.

"Dr. Brown," Samuel gasped. "It's me, Samuel."

It was as if the name caused something in the doctor to click, and he suddenly released Samuel, who gasped and coughed.

"I'm sorry," Dr. Brown muttered, "I must've been dreaming." He backed away, brushed his fingers through his hair, which barely improved its wild look, then covered his mouth.

"It's okay," Samuel soothed. "Why don't we sit down?"

Dr. Brown nodded, then noticed Mary. "Who is she?"

"This is Mary," Samuel said. "She's a friend. She's been giving you all this food. You said that you had wanted to thank her. Well, here she is."

Dr. Brown stared at Mary suspiciously, warily. The circles under his eyes were so dark that Mary thought she might get lost in them. Up until then, she had not moved from her spot beside the door.

"I hope you don't mind me coming along," Mary managed, trying to keep her voice from shaking. "I've been wanting to meet you."

"You were the girl selling produce," Dr. Brown said.

Mary recognized him. She had seen those sapphire eyes before. "Yes." She thrust her hands forward and announced, "I've brought some muffins, freshly baked this morning." Her words suddenly inspired her to give him a kitten.

Dr. Brown's eyes lit up as he took Mary's basket. He helped himself to a muffin, savoring it with a moan and a smile. Samuel turned to Mary and smiled.

"*Danki,*" he whispered.

'For what?" Mary asked.

"For being so kind to him. I know that he looks bad, but he isn't always like this."

Mary nodded and smiled, but it wasn't a genuine smile because, in her heart, she knew that Dr. Brown could not remain in that room, but she had no idea how to tell Samuel.

CHAPTER 4: BRAVE
IN HER EYES

"Goodbye, Dr. Brown," Mary said. "I hope to see you again soon."

"Goodbye, Mary. And thank you for the food."

Mary smiled and nodded as she stepped out of the door.

"I'll try and come again later," Samuel promised.

"I'll be fine," Dr. Brown assured him.

Samuel closed the door and turned the key. He turned to Mary. "I can't believe how quickly he warmed to you."

Mary said nothing. It had taken a good part of the afternoon to get Dr. Brown comfortable with Mary's presence, and it was only in the last half-an-hour that he stopped throwing her suspicious looks.

"I think he looked a lot better this afternoon," Samuel noted. "He ate something at least."

Mary could hear the hope in Samuel's voice, and it made her want to wrap her arms around him. She knew how much he wanted Dr. Brown to be better, but the truth was that the man was far from fine. Mary had spent all afternoon observing him, and it was clear that he had some mental condition that distressed him.

"Can I walk you to the road?" Samuel offered.

Mary accepted, and they began to walk south, across the meadow. "Was he that thin when you first met him?" She could not get the image of Dr. Brown out of her mind. The hollows of his cheeks and his frail frame conjured the image of a scarecrow she and Rachel had dressed once in their father's clothes. They had been much too big, so he had looked as if he were drowning in fabric. It had been a funny sight to see when the man was made of straw. However, it was the furthest thing from humorous in a man of flesh and bone.

Samuel hesitated and then shook his head. "He lost some weight, but I'm sure that with your delicious cooking, he'll be back to his old self in no time."

Mary frowned. She was worried about Dr. Brown, but she was worried about Samuel as well. He was deluding himself into thinking that he could fix the doctor when it was evident that Dr. Brown needed more help than either of them could give him.

When they reached the road, Mary and Samuel stopped. Mary had to tell Samuel how she felt.

"Samuel, I need to say something."

"Wait," Samuel interjected. "Before you do, there is something I want to say first."

Mary waited.

"I want to say *danki*, for everything. I'm not sure that I would've been able to do this without you. Caring for Dr. Brown has been one of the hardest things that I have ever done, but knowing you are here to help makes the burden a hundred times lighter."

Mary looked up into Samuel's face, and she saw the gratitude in his smile and the optimism in his eyes. She knew that if she said what she felt, it would crush him, and she didn't have the heart to do that, at least not then.

"I'm glad I can help, Sam," Mary said. "It's late, and I'd better be going."

"Of course," Samuel said, frowning slightly. "I'll see you soon?"

Mary nodded and then hurried away from Samuel, not turning around as she walked toward home. As soon as she was far enough not to be heard, she allowed a sob to escape her chest. The events of the afternoon had been overwhelming, and the emotion that Mary had held back now came rushing to the surface. Hot tears spilled down her cheeks, blurring her vision and leaving a trail as she walked, her world suddenly wrought with sadness.

Mary slept poorly. She wrestled with her conscience like Jacob with the angel of the Lord, but morning light brought her no blessing, only the conviction that others ought to know about Dr. Brown. But whom could she tell? She dressed and hurried downstairs to focus on the morning's chores. That would keep her distracted. When breakfast was over and the washing up had been done, Mary put on her thick shawl and *kapp* and headed out of the house to the King farm. Her steps were determined; she walked with purpose and a resolve that must not waver. *Will not waver*, she repeated to herself like a mantra. At the gate, the new issue of finding the farm boy interrupted her train of thought. The barn would be the logical choice. And, indeed, that was where she found Samuel, murmuring to the animals, half soothing them about his presence, half chiding them for their mess. Mary stepped into the barn.

Samuel turned around. "Mary! What're you doing here?"

Mary's smile faltered like it had stepped onto the red carpet at the rink only to have it slip on the ice beneath it. It tumbled off of her face. She had felt so brave walking over, walking quickly to catch up to her confidence racing before her. But after seeing Samuel, doubt had taken the lead.

"What's wrong?" Samuel asked. Mary's face presaged bad news. He put down his pail and leaned in. "Has something happened? Is someone hurt?"

Mary shook her head. "No. It's nothing like that."

"Then what is it?"

Mary hesitated.

"Mary. You're scaring me."

Mary exhaled. "Sam, I need to talk to you about Dr. Brown."

Samuel frowned. "What is it?"

Mary noticed Samuel's face. They had spent so little of their time together and had been unable to bask in each others' company. Either they had been avoiding the Weavers' prying eyes or taking care of Dr. Brown. This was her first chance to actually pause and contemplate his face, and it looked worn. Purplish bags lay under his eyes, providing the only color to his snowman complexion. It was clear to her that both men needed her help, and being men, they were about as likely to ask for it as they were to ask for directions. At once, she felt resolute. She had to do this not only for Dr. Brown, but for Sam too.

"Dr. Brown needs help, Sam."

"We are helping him," Samuel replied.

Mary shook her head. "What he needs is real help before it's too late. We are in way over our heads, Samuel."

Samuel exhaled sharply. "I should never have taken you to

see him. It was a mistake." He turned away from Mary and continued to feed the animals.

"It wasn't a mistake," Mary insisted. "I needed to see for myself. Ever since you told me about Dr. Brown, I've been unable to reconcile how I felt about the situation. I wanted to help you so badly, Sam, that I tried to ignore how serious the situation sounded. But then, yesterday, when I saw him, I could no longer pretend."

Samuel still would not look at Mary. "He's not always that bad," he said weakly.

"Look at me, Samuel," Mary insisted. He turned around but stared past Mary at a spot on the barn wall.

"You need to stop lying to yourself. I know that you're trying to protect Dr. Brown, but by doing that, you are denying the truth. He is a sick man, Sam, and he needs our help." Without thinking, she reached over and took his hand in hers. It was rough and dusty, but Mary squeezed it gently.

Mary then whispered, "I think we should speak to my *daed*."

Samuel frowned at the thought.

"I've been thinking all night about who we can ask for help. It needs to be someone who will hear us when we speak and be compassionate and understanding. I think my *daed* is the right person to tell. I know the *Amisch* don't associate with outsiders, but if we frame it as some sort of experiment to my *daed*, he'll be open-minded." Mary waited for Samuel to speak, still holding his hand in hers.

Samuel looked at her. "You're right," he sighed. "Dr. Brown needs more help than I can give him, but I'm terrified, Mary. Over the last few days, I've seen his condition deteriorate, and I've been too scared to admit to myself that he's getting worse.

At first, I thought it was because I was protecting him, but now I realize that I was afraid to admit that I haven't changed. I'm the same stupid, proud, foolish man I was before I left."

The bitterness in Samuel's voice shocked Mary. None of what he had just revealed had ever crossed her mind, and she was astounded how someone could be so wrong about himself.

"You don't know yourself at all, do you?" Mary asked gently. "Just because you could not admit to yourself that Dr. Brown needed help does not make you foolish; it makes you human. It makes you someone who is compassionate and kind and who puts the needs of someone else above your own. Your time away did you good. The day you arrived on our front porch, I knew you were not the same person you were before. I saw quiet confidence and a big heart. When you asked for my help, I considered it a privilege to have your confidence. So, I extend to you the same courtesy. I have confidence in you. The last time I confronted you with something important, you didn't let me down. Asking for help, now, is not about admitting defeat or looking weak and foolish. You just think you're superhuman because you're big and strong." She rubbed her hands along his arm muscles, suddenly exhilarated by his physique, then pulled away lest she sin. "It's about being brave enough to put all of that aside and help a man who is dangling at the edge of a precipice. Forgive yourself for your past and realize that you are better than you think."

Samuel gazed into her eyes. No one had ever looked at him like Mary was right then. It was a look of love and pride, one he had always yearned to see. "You don't think I'm weak?" Samuel whispered. "Weak" had been his father's choice word to describe his son, and the spiny bur had stuck to the farm boy's heart.

With the nimble hands of a seamstress, Mary cupped his face

in hers and said, "I think that you need to find the courage to see who you truly are and to stop seeing yourself through the eyes of others." The bur fell to the floor, and Mary took its place on Samuel's heart.

"In your eyes, I am brave," Samuel murmured.

Mary nodded, then whispered, "In my eyes, you are everything you could ever hope to be and everything you could ever want to be."

Samuel's world stopped turning. All pretense fell away. He stood before her, exposed to his very soul, and she had found him fitting. His one desire was to please her. He leaned into her. She closed her eyes. Then, the barn doors swung open.

"Hello!"

"Thomas!" Mary exclaimed, her heart still beating in her ears. "What are you doing here?"

"Hannah promised I could come for a riding lesson. Mr. King just got a new pony who is the perfect size for me, and when Hannah came over for tea yesterday, she promised Rachel that I could come for a ride."

Mary nodded. "That's nice, Thomas, but Hannah is not here," Mary said.

Thomas looked around the barn. "Any idea where she is?"

"Try the house," Samuel said dryly.

Thomas nodded and skipped out of the barn. Despite herself, Mary grinned, then giggled, then roared with laughter. Finally, Samuel smiled too.

"Thomas has an awful habit of popping up at the most inconvenient times," Mary quipped. She wiped the tears from her eyes but could not stop laughing. The emotions from the risk of being caught in a near kiss were escaping from the girl, overwhelming her with joy. To top it off, Samuel understood her. He listened to her and responded. She felt light yet mighty at having turned such a hunk of a man to her point of view. Once she regained her composure, she was quick to get back on track. "Will you come to my house this afternoon?" she asked in a syrupy tone. "We can speak to my *daed* together."

Samuel nodded, still smarting from the missed opportunity. How could he refuse? The lips he had desired were now stretched in the sweetest smile. He didn't dare do anything to wipe it off of her face. "I'll come after lunch."

Mary then pressed up onto her toes and kissed Samuel gently on the cheek. "It'll be okay. I promise."

CHAPTER 5: A RUDE REACQUAINTANCE

Levi King was not a nice man. He hated change. He despised anything new, and he especially detested losing control. Tradition, the tried-and-true, was where his heart was. Why be so arrogant as to create something new? He had forgotten that his anger at being rejected fueled his unruly character. Remorse is a bitter fuel that burns dark and whose smoke blinds. It had been decades since Levi King had seen clearly. What he craved were attention and praise. He had figured that he would get it when his strapping son married the bishop's daughter, but when she had rejected him for the son of his one-time fiancée, he had turned on his own son. Levi nagged and taunted Samuel for being weak. He blamed his son for his rejection and took it personally; it was an insult to his upbringing and, thus, to Levi himself. He did not admit that he hated himself for having raised a boy who would suffer rejection as he had suffered. If he had, he would have indicted himself. As it was, he blamed everyone else for things not to his liking.

Rachel was flighty, unreliable, and easily manipulated, Levi concluded. Noah was a thief who should have stayed where he came from in Ohio. Everything was perfect until he returned to visit Isaiah. Oh! Isaiah, of the stock who gave up on commitments. What a shameful family heritage! *It served him right to have his wife die,* Levi thought. Of course, Levi King was not so foolish as to share these thoughts with others. Instead, he used them for fuel to interact with the other Amish, who, in his own eyes, were inferior in the faith to himself since he was the one made to suffer for their unfaithfulness. Were it not for his rancor and misery, he would not speak to a soul. For what is there to say to those who cannot recognize genius?

When Isaiah had agreed to help Levi with winter chores on the King farm, the latter expected him to be good for it. When Isaiah was hospitalized, Levi assumed Isaiah would send Noah or some other person from his farm to help and fulfill his promise. When no word came from Isaiah to explain why he had reneged on his commitment, Levi took offense. Now that Isaiah had returned, he was more than willing to help a widowed hussy (Levi used pejorative *Englischer* words only to himself). He was infuriated. How could this woman command Isaiah's attention when he owed her nothing? Had his family not shamed Levi—twice— and didn't Isaiah feel himself obliged to make up for it? It would have been the right thing to do, in Levi's eyes. Alas! the Kings were slighted yet again.

When Levi came upon Isaiah and Adel at the market, he ignored them. He was angry with his son, appalled at his *Englischer* school courses, and indignant that the boy was not keen to farm. Instead, he was always taking walks. *I could have used him for this trip to the market,* he thought.

"Hello, Levi," Isaiah offered. "I'd like for you to meet Adel."

The store was too small for Levi to pass off as though he hadn't heard them, so he mumbled his answer, turned on his heel, and went outside for a walk. Isaiah's blood boiled, for Levi had made it a habit to slight him at church and about the community. Adel's hand on his arm, however, soothed him. He decided not to chase after the man, choosing instead to pay for his things and be on his way.

In the buggy, Isaiah interpreted the scene to Adel. "That's Levi King. My sister was engaged to him but left him for another man in Ohio. He's never forgiven her for it. Noah's her son. Rachel was supposed to marry Levi's son, Samuel, but chose my kin instead. Now he hates our whole family. He's—" Isaiah paused to choose his words wisely, "—difficult."

"That explains why he drove past me."

"What are you talking about?"

Adel's eyes widened. Her heart raced, thumping its beat in her temples. She had said too much. Isaiah waited. "Oh, it was nothing."

"Adel." The look on his face said the rest, that he didn't believe her, and that she ought to explain.

"Let's talk and ride," Adel suggested.

They mounted the buggy and were on their way. Adel said nothing. Isaiah, savvy to her trick, spoke up. "What are you talking about?" Adel looked to Isaiah, then back to her hands. She swallowed. She played with her fingers. Isaiah could hardly concentrate on the road. "Adel?"

"I saw him one day on the side of the road. He stopped to look at me, shook his head, then went away."

"I don't understand. How did what I just told you make that scene make sense? What did you say to him?"

Adel looked to Isaiah. He glanced at her. Apprehension was all he could see in her, though he could not yet tell if she was afraid of Levi or of his own reaction. She looked to her fingers, regretting having said anything.

"What did you say to him?"

Adel flopped her hands onto her lap as though she were done with them, then threw her hands up half-heartedly, and answered, "I asked him for help."

"Help with what?

Adel picked at her nails. She waved her hands about like she didn't know what to do with them, "Help with—" she went back to her fingers—"I was in labor."

"What?"

With her head bowed, Adel nodded.

"He did what?" The buggy veered left when Isaiah put his hand on his hip as he turned to Adel. He quickly regained control of the reins. "How long were you there for?"

"I don't know. I'm just glad you came along."

"He didn't help you?" Isaiah bit his tongue. *I'm not a bit surprised,* he thought. *That scoundrel! That no good, rotten, unchivalrous—*"Ahh!" he yelled, frustrated that he could not continue his mental diatribe.

"But I'm okay now." Adel's words had no effect. Her escort gritted his teeth with a clenched jaw.

"That was an affront to everything we stand for! You could have died! And for what? For what my sister did to him years ago?" At the intersection, Isaiah made a U-turn.

"Where are you going?"

"To have a chat with my old friend."

"You're not going to confront him, are you?"

"He had better have a good excuse for what he did."

"Isaiah! No! You can't! It isn't proper."

"If a man has sinned, go out and point out his fault, just the two of you. It's the first step, Adel."

"Oh! Isaiah. I don't want to be involved."

"Stay in the buggy." Isaiah hurried inside. "Where's Levi?"

"He's gone; he left shortly after you did."

Isaiah hurried back to his buggy.

"Where are we going?"

"To his farm."

"Oh, no! I told you that I didn't want to be involved, so take me home first."

Isaiah sighed. He pulled the reins, "Whoa!" then turned to Adel. "Look, what he did, that's not right. It's a sin. He must be held accountable."

"I told you, I don't want trouble."

"You were lying on the road just outside of his farm! It was a stone's throw to take you home and have his wife help you!"

Adel sat arms crossed, looking straight ahead. Isaiah stared at her, incredulous that she was unoffended by Levi's heartless act. He sighed again, loudly. She understood his displeasure. "I find it a breach of trust to confront him on something that's long past."

"But it's a sin! Remember the parable of the Good Samaritan?"

"I know the story, Isaiah. It's your temper that I'm afraid of."

Isaiah hung his head. He did not want to disappoint her, but his sense of duty—of manhood—compelled him to act on her behalf. "What if I go with someone else?"

"Like whom?"

Isaiah turned away as though the answer might be found over his shoulder. "The bishop! He'd be perfect. I can drop you off right now and head over there."

"It's lunchtime. Wait until we've had ours. Besides, I like having you at the table with me." Adel smiled, and Isaiah relented lest his heart melt.

"Deal," Isaiah said.

CHAPTER 6: SCARS

Lunchtime was slow to arrive for Mary. The whole situation had her distracted, so she could not sit still for more than a few moments.

"For goodness' sake, Mary," Mrs. Lapp chided. "You are as bad as that kitten, skittering this way and that. If you can't concentrate on your needlework, then go for a walk."

Mary smiled sheepishly and did as her mother suggested. She ambled around the yard for an hour until she was called in to help set the table for lunch. Mary nervously laid out the plates and cutlery. Despite her assurances to Samuel, she was concerned about her father's reaction to their confession. While she knew that he would not behave rashly or be inconsiderate toward Dr. Brown, her father may be angry that they had kept a secret.

Finally, there was a knock at the door. Mary kept her head down. Bishop Lapp got up from the table and walked the narrow passage toward the door. "Samuel," he said warmly. "What a nice surprise! Please come in." Bishop Lapp returned to the kitchen with Samuel, who smiled at Mary and Mrs. Lapp. She noticed that his smile did not quite reach his eyes, and Mary knew that Samuel was feeling as apprehensive as she was about speaking to her father.

"Samuel," Mrs. Lapp said. "We heard you were back. How

lovely for you to come by and visit. We have just finished lunch, but I can put a plate together for you if you're hungry."

"That is very kind of you, Mrs. Lapp, but I'm afraid that my visit is not a social one. I'm here to speak to Bishop Lapp about a rather serious matter."

Bishop Lapp and Mrs. Lapp looked at each other, then looked gravely at their guest.

"If you have a moment, would you speak with me?" Samuel asked, looking at Mary's father.

"Of course," Bishop Lapp said. "Come to my study, and we can talk."

"Actually, *Daed*, we both need to talk to you."

Again, Bishop Lapp and Mrs. Lapp looked at one another.

"Then let's all go into the living room," Bishop Lapp suggested.

The quartet retired to the living room where Mrs. Lapp shooed a sleeping Muffin off the chair and directed Samuel toward it. The kitten gave them all a disgruntled look before leaving the room. Bishop Lapp looked from Mary to Samuel.

"What is it you wanted to talk to me about?"

Samuel cleared his throat. "Bishop, a week ago I visited your home, and I spoke to Mary." Samuel recounted the entire story. The Lapps sat and listened, growing more concerned with each new detail revealed. "This morning, Mary found me and convinced me that we needed to tell someone. She thought that you would be the best person to tell and that you might help Dr. Brown. I was unsure at first, but she made me see that it was the right thing to do. I trust you, Sir."

Mary held her breath. She hoped that telling her father would be the right decision. She bit her lip waiting for her father to respond.

"This is a very worrying story," Bishop Lapp said. "I'm still unsure as to why you decided to take the man into your home Samuel. But you have done the right thing by telling me. I need to see Dr. Brown at once." His urgency shocked the youths, but they figured to delay him was futile.

Samuel bowed his head and looked at his hands. "I brought the buggy. I can drive us over there now."

"Mary must stay behind," Mrs. Lapp said.

"But *Maem*, I must go."

"From what you have told us, Dr. Brown sounds unhinged, poor soul. He could be a danger to you."

Mary opened her mouth to argue, but Samuel interjected. "I would not let anything bad happen to Mary, Mrs. Lapp. And Dr. Brown trusts her as he would a friend. I think that her presence would be helpful."

Mrs. Lapp looked at her husband.

"I'll make sure she's safe," Bishop Lapp promised his wife.

They hurried out of the house before the bishop's wife could conjure up any more objections. They mounted the buggy and rode quietly to the Kings' farm. Mary alternated glances at Samuel and her father. They sat solemn-faced and entranced by the confrontation that awaited them. Samuel tensed his jaw just as his farm came into view. This conflict, for him, was between the faith of his upbringing and the faith of the English. The Jesus they offered him inspired him, whilst the Amish Jesus, he felt, held him in a strait jacket. His thoughts oscillated between helping the poor doctor and weighing the chances of his shunning.

"I'll park the buggy here, and we can walk down."

Bishop Lapp nodded. Samuel climbed down from the buggy

and looked about, spying for his father. *I don't need my old man to make matters worse,* he thought, using the colloquial *Englischer* term to which his kind would surely object. Pejorative terms were forbidden in Amish country, yet it expressed exactly how he felt about his father. Even now, he begrudged his father for being short-fused and intolerant. How he wished he could have turned to him for help rather than Mary's dad! Once at the cottage, Samuel took one more look around before he removed the small key from his pocket.

Bishop Lapp frowned. "You keep him locked in?"

"It's for his safety," Samuel said. Just before he pushed open the door, Samuel paused and turned to them both. "Let me go in first to prepare him." They nodded. Samuel pushed open the door.

"Dr. Brown?" Samuel called. "It's me, Samuel."

There was no sound inside the cottage. Mary's stomach sank to the floor. What if something had happened to him?

Then, a loud crash was followed by shouting. Samuel rushed inside with the bishop close behind. Mary straggled behind in no hurry to witness the scene. The noise came from the tiny bedroom at the opposite end of the cottage. Dr. Brown stood on the small bed stripped of its linen. There were streaks of blood across the mattress. A small gas lantern lay shattered on the floor, its glass spread to every corner of the matchbox-sized space. A wooden chair lay broken in one corner of the room, its front legs splintered, with the seat lying on the bed. The doctor stopped shouting, now muttering something under his breath.

"What is he saying?" the bishop asked.

"The same thing he always says," Samuel whispered. "Hassan, I'm sorry. I'm sorry, Hassan. He must be dreaming."

Dr. Brown had not noticed them. He stared at the blank wall

before him with eyes glazed and unfocused. Unsteady on his feet, he rocked back and forth at once to find his balance and to self-soothe. Mary worried that he would fall off the bed and onto the glass.

"Dr. Brown," Samuel pleaded. "Please come down before you hurt yourself."

Dr. Brown did not move, and when Samuel attempted to reach for him, he viciously swatted at him. Samuel took a step back, assessing whether the man was still asleep. The bishop was composed. Like a cat on high alert, his senses were attuned to the entirety of their surroundings. He seemed, strange at it may sound, tensely at ease, ready to flee danger yet unmoved by fear.

"Dr. Brown," Bishop Lapp said kindly. "You don't know me, but my name is Bishop Lapp, and I am here to help you."

"Who are you? What are they doing here?" Dr. Brown yelled.

"Samuel wanted you to meet me. I'm Mary's father."

Dr. Brown blinked several times, then reckoned that he was no longer ensnared in his nightmare. "I apologize for the scene. I think that I was having a nightmare."

"You were looking for Hassan?" the bishop inquired.

"Yes."

"I'm sorry to be the bearer of bad news, Doctor, but Hassan is dead."

Dr. Brown sobbed. Years of stagnant tears, embittered by the poisonous tea of remorse and self-loathing, cascaded from the doctor's dark ringed eyes, overwhelming his ducts so that they were forced to seep from his nose and his mouth. His ears would have wept if it meant relieving his pain. Samuel hugged him. The doctor sobbed for a long time. None rushed him to its end, for the Amish are a patient people. It was evident to the trio around

Dr. Brown that the moment was profound—none could grasp its depth. It was some time before a break in the wailing afforded Bishop Lapp a chance to find out.

"It is important to remember those whom we've lost in order to properly mourn them. Please, tell us about Hassan."

Dr. Brown sniffled, wiped his face with his left sleeve, then the right, before taking a deep breath. "He helped me around the field hospital. He'd get my medical supplies—bandages, gauze, things of that sort. He'd help with the triage—girls on one side, boys on the other. He'd direct them with a smile, proud of his status. He was quite good at it. He couldn't speak English, but he wanted to learn. He knew all of the things, but the people..." He didn't finish the sentence. "He knew 'boy' and 'girl' and 'doctor.' My goodness, he was cute." Dr. Brown paused, likely recalling the boy's face. "He'd say the strangest things. One day, he walked in with a woman holding a baby. He was sad but keen for me to see the infant. I asked him if the baby with him was his baby brother. He learned to say it, but he kept repeating, 'baby brother' whenever I treated a baby—any baby! I don't know if they were related." Dr. Brown smiled for the first time, a true, genuine grin with eyes lit up. "One day, I was treating a baby girl for burn wounds—" his smile disappeared likely due to the mental image. "Hassan pointed to her and said, 'girl baby brother,' and he handed me a diaper." He giggled. Dr. Brown broke out into a sympathetic laugh, as one does when reminded of a happy moment during a tragedy.

Mary giggled at the story while the men bowed their heads and swallowed hard.

"I couldn't protect Hassan." Dr. Brown cried for over an hour, a cleansing weep to rinse him of his sorrow and trauma. The bishop had the wherewithal to offer him some water lest dehydration compound the tragedy before them.

"How did he die?"

The three men turned to look at Mary. Dr. Brown held his breath and sucked in his lips. Samuel and her father both looked like they were trying to think of what to say. Mary blushed, embarrassed that she had been enraptured by the story and had let it get the better of her.

Dr. Brown opened his mouth, but Levi King's voice boomed out. "Samuel? What's going on in here? What's the meaning of this?" Then, to Dr. Brown, "Who are you? You're not Amish. You can't be here." Levi's heavy steps carried him up the porch and into the small abode intended for his farm manager.

Samuel turned to face his father, angry with himself for having left the cottage door open. Surely, had it been closed, it would not have aroused his father's suspicion. Dr. Brown flexed every muscle in preparation to flee or fight. Mary covered her mouth and the gasp that came out of it. Her father stepped forward, about to explain. Another voice could be heard from outside.

"Levi King? I've got a bone to pick with you!" It was Isaiah Fisher.

The farmer King turned to face his nemesis, blocking the doorway and keeping him outside. "Oh, yeah? I'm sure what I did wasn't as bad as what your family has been doing to me."

Isaiah marched up the little porch and stood chest to chest with Levi, then looked up into his eyes, he being the shorter of the two. "Adel told me what you did to her."

"I haven't so much as talked to her since she arrived."

"You left her by the side of the road when she was in labor!"

"Ha! That's a fine lie. I never saw her."

"She saw you look at her and shake your head!"

"Isaiah?" said the doctor.

Isaiah froze. He recognized the voice. "Andrew?" He pushed past Levi.

"So, you know this imposter too?" Levi spat.

"Andrew! What are you doing here?"

"It's a long story. How's your baby?"

Isaiah stared blankly at the man who'd hit him with his truck. "My baby?" And then it clicked. "Leora? How do you know about her?"

Levi was seething. "Can someone please explain to me what on earth is going on here?" He glared at all in the cottage, his ire especially reserved for Samuel.

"Levi," Bishop Lapp began, "we will explain everything, but first, I need to ask you to calm down. You are scaring everyone." His words had the opposite effect, Levi's face turning the shade of puce.

"Don't tell me to calm down. My cottage is being used to harbor some kind of *Englisch* fugitive, and you expect me to do what? Sit down and drink tea with him?"

"Dr. Brown is not an *Englisch* fugitive, but he is a very sick man, so if you could retain some composure, it would be much appreciated," the bishop advised.

Levi King's gaze moved to Dr. Brown, who was pale but otherwise lucid. "Who is that man?" he asked, pointing at the *Englischer*.

"His name is Dr. Andrew Brown, and he's my friend," Samuel said.

Father looked at son with a mixture of surprise and disappointment. He opened his mouth, but before he could speak,

Bishop Lapp interjected.

"There will be plenty of time to explain everything, but right now, we need to get Dr. Brown some help."

Ignoring Levi's glare, Bishop Lapp turned to Mary. "Mary, please go and gather up all of Dr. Brown's things, and then I think we should go."

Mary nodded and went off to the bedroom where she put all of Dr. Brown's belongings in a suitcase found under the bed. The disquieting silence in the next room was worse than the ranting. Mary returned to the men as quickly as she could, only to be stopped dead in her tracks, such was the tension in the air. She waited for one of them to move before walking out in their wake.

"Is that everything?" Bishop Lapp asked.

"I think so," Mary said.

"*Gut*, then let us take our leave. Dr. Brown, will you come with us?"

Andrew looked at the bishop, then at Isaiah. Bishop Lapp made eye contact with Isaiah, and the two understood to whose house they would go.

Isaiah looked to the *Englischer*, gestured toward the door, and said, "Follow me."

Andrew nodded and walked toward the door with the Lapps and Samuel in tow.

"Samuel, where do you think you are going?" Levi demanded.

Samuel turned around.

"I am going with Dr. Brown."

"You certainly are not," Levi snapped.

"But *Daed*, I must. Dr. Brown trusts me, and he needs my help."

Unadulterated rage flashed across Levi's face.

"Samuel," the bishop said softly, "I think you should listen to your *daed*. Dr. Brown will be safe with us. I promise that we will take care of him."

Samuel nodded. "*Danki*, for everything. You've been like a father to me."

The quartet galloped out of the cottage.

CHAPTER 7: FATHER AND SON

"**S**amuel," Levi said.

Samuel said nothing.

"Samuel, look at me," Levi instructed. Samuel sighed and turned to his father.

"Why have you been hiding an *Englisch* doctor here?"

"Is there any point in explaining myself? Nothing I say or do has ever given you a favorable opinion of me, so should I waste my breath trying to explain?"

Levi frowned at his son, but, miraculously, held his tongue. Father and son had a complicated relationship, but the physical distance between them over the past two years could have brought them closer together. Levi, at least, had secretly hoped for it, though things looked bleak since Samuel had been distant. Levi now realized that Andrew was the reason why. "You said that man was your friend," Levi said as calmly as he could. "How did you come to form such a friendship?"

Samuel gave an exasperated sigh. "Of course, you could not understand how someone would choose to be friends with the *Englisch*. You know nothing of the world outside or what it means to be a part of it."

Levi inhaled. His son's petulance grated against his temper. "I respect the *Englisch*, but they do not share our beliefs or our way of life. I'm concerned at how this friendship with an outsider caused you to lie and to steal from your own family."

"Dr. Brown never asked me to," Samuel said. "I chose to make those decisions because I knew that if I asked for your help, you would refuse."

"You are always so ready to paint me the villain, Samuel, which is a convenient way of relieving yourself of the onus of responsibility. *You* chose to bring this man onto our farm and to lie to us. First the incident with the Miller boy, and now this mad *Englisch* doctor? When will you grow up and stop making such rash decisions? You have a brain in your head. Use it."

Samuel said nothing, choosing instead to stare at his boots. His father had a point, but he had insulted his manhood when he threw the incident with Noah Miller in his face. Out of jealously of Noah and his budding friendship with Rachel, Samuel's fiancée at the time, Samuel had locked Noah in a coal shed right before a blizzard. Noah had almost died. Samuel did not like to be reminded of his immature prank, so he inhaled to keep his cool. "You're right. I'm the one who brought Dr. Brown here, and I'm sorry for lying to you and for stealing food. I only did it because he had nowhere else to go, but you wouldn't understand."

"Why wouldn't I?" Levi asked.

"Because you don't recognize weakness as a part of human nature," Samuel cried. "You see any sign of fragility as a fatal flaw that must be beaten back lest you die. My whole life, I've been terrified of showing you the smallest hint of vulnerability because I did not want you to feel ashamed of me. You still haven't forgiven me for what I did to Noah Miller or for letting Rachel go. You think I'm weak, and that's why I knew that I could never bring a broken *Englisch* man to your door because you would have received him with contempt and scorn."

Levi was ashamed, for there, Samuel spoke the truth. Levi had been raised by a hard man, much harder than himself. It had, in turn, shaped him as a father. He had not planned to throw the Miller incident in Samuel's face again, but he could not take it back now. "I know that I've been hard on you, Samuel, but it's my responsibility to make sure you are a man of worth and substance."

"According to who?" Samuel asked.

Levi exhaled. He could see that Samuel was hurt, but he had no idea how to fix what was broken between them. The truth was that he had never known. "You don't want to tell me the story of the *Englisch* doctor, but I want to hear it. So, forget your feelings toward me for a few minutes and tell me how you came to be friends with this man."

Samuel looked to his father to gauge his sincerity. Once satisfied, he spoke. Levi listened to the strange story of how a young, Amish man had stumbled upon a sick *English* doctor and offered him shelter, and from there, an unexpected friendship had grown. It was a tale of kindness, compassion, and understanding, and when Samuel had finished, Levi found himself speechless. Throughout Samuel's story, Levi had searched for one small thing to hold onto, something he could relate to or understand, but there was nothing. He was unsure how he had raised a man so unlike himself and his father. Levi struggled to find the right words. When he did, he could only whisper them. "I'm sorry that you felt you could not tell me about Dr. Brown."

"So am I," Samuel said.

"I hoped that as you grew older, we might find some common ground. I know that when you decided to go to the city, I was not as supportive as I should have been. I hoped that the time away would make you see how much you missed the farm and make you realize that leaving was a mistake. But I see now that perhaps I was naïve to think time apart would heal what was broken between us."

"Distance is rarely a way to bring people back together again, especially if they are oceans apart," Samuel said.

"I think I'm beginning to see that now," Levi retorted.

The sun sank beyond the hills, and the air smelled of wood fires.

"So where do we go from here?" Levi asked.

Samuel shrugged.

"Are you coming back home?"

"I haven't decided yet."

"Well, I don't know if it's worth anything, but I want you here on the farm," Levi said. "You're a King, and you're my son, and this land is where you belong."

Samuel nodded but said nothing more.

"I also want you to know that while I may disagree with your methods, in the end, you did the right thing, helping that man. It was what a good Christian man would have done, and I'm glad you are that if nothing else."

Samuel knew his father intended his words to be a compliment, but like most things he said, it was double-edged, and they left a bitter taste in Samuel's mouth. Father and son stood side by side at the edge of the porch to watch the last of the golden sunshine pour across the hills and bare trees. A passerby never would have guessed that a chasm stood between them.

"Let's go home," Levi said.

Samuel nodded, and he followed his father down the porch steps toward the house. The sun had set by the time they reached the house, revealing a starless sky.

"*Daed*," Samuel said. "I know we still have a lot to talk about, but I need to find out what happened with Dr. Brown."

Levi nodded. "Go. We'll talk more later."

CHAPTER 8: GETTING REACQUAINTED

The quartet headed to the Miller farm, Isaiah and Andrew leading the way, sharing about what had happened to each of them since they had last spoken. Mary walked beside her father, curious as to his method of intervention.

"How did you know about Hassan?" Mary asked.

"Isaiah told me," Bishop Lapp explained.

The look on Mary's face conveyed to her father that, should his intention have been to bring clarity, he had only muddied the waters.

"I'd heard the name before. When I went to visit him in the hospital before he was released, he told me about a man haunted by the civil war in Syria, particularly about the children. The name *Hassan* had only been mentioned once by Isaiah, but I still recognized it when I heard it again. Dr. Brown had been visiting Isaiah but then had stopped coming. He told me that he was concerned about him and that perhaps he was unwell. I inquired with the hospital staff, but they, too, said that they had not seen him for some time. Perhaps it was naïve of me, but I thought maybe Dr. Brown had sought out treatment for his condition."

"You know what is wrong with him?" Mary asked.

"After what Isaiah told me, I suspected that he might have PTSD," Bishop Lapp said.

"What's that?"

"Post-Traumatic Stress Disorder," Bishop Lapp explained.

The same *you've muddied the waters* look appeared on Mary's face.

"It happens to anyone whose body or mind has undergone severe trauma. When Dr. Brown worked in Syria, the prolonged traumatic experience left him with deep emotional scars."

"Can he be cured?"

"There is no simple cure for PTSD. What he has to do is relive those moments in his mind until he is desensitized to them. It can take years. The *Englisch* have therapists, people paid to listen and to care."

"How do you know all of this, *Daed*?" Mary asked.

"I am a man of many interests, Mary." He smiled at his youngest. "When I was a boy, some of our folk were sued by the *Englisch* and went to prison for refusing to fight in the Vietnam War. Though I thought that it was unjust, the stories I heard about the returning *Englisch* led me to conclude that our folk had not been so unfortunate. The soldiers came among us carrying the war in their hearts. They sought peace in our ways and hoped to find who they had once been. It was then that I started reading about the human mind and its complexities."

"When do you have time for that?"

"My goodness, *Dochder*, what do you think I do in my study?"

Mary had never fathomed that her father was informed. As a result, she was pensive for the rest of the way, occasionally looking at her father with a mixture of awe and fascination. There was much she had to learn.

Isaiah and Andrew were aware of the Lapps' conversation, but had struck up their own, so they were not paying attention.

"How did you meet Hassan?" Isaiah asked.

"I was working for Doctors Without Borders." Andrew stopped talking to hold back the tears. When he spoke again, his voice quivered. "It's been a long time since I've known any kind of peace. When I sleep, all I can dream about are the horrors of war. I hear screams. I am haunted by those who I could not save and by those whom I'd saved but were later lost in the fighting. Hassan is why I moved here. I found him hiding under a sink. I mended his wounds—some minor cuts—and gave him part of my lunch. He took a liking to me, so much so that he followed me everywhere, like a shadow. He was a gentle and kind boy, and I took him under my wing." Andrew's hands trembled.

Isaiah waited.

"Hassan became a fixture in the hospital, endearing himself to all. He befriended the Violet (an NGO) ambulance staff who let him sit in their ambulance. He was hiding in there when they answered a call. Bombers had taken out a neighborhood; his ambulance responded, and then the bombers returned to bomb the same place with the paramedics there. They lost two trucks and three paramedics that day. Hassan, too. I've seen burn victims before, but hardly ever before *and* after, and never a child. Seeing him dead and disfigured was my toughest loss. I had to leave. If I hadn't left, then I would've been swallowed whole by the grief and the madness. I hoped that being stateside would quiet the screaming inside my head, but the city is bright and loud. I needed to go somewhere quiet, so I moved to Erie. But then we met."

Andrew's breathing was shaky. He wanted to both cry and

wail at once, but each suppressed the other. Thus, an eerie calm overcame him. "I thought that leaving Syria would help me to forget Hassan especially, but he is still walking behind me. My little shadow."

Isaiah kept his eyes before him rather than turning to look at the haunted man walking beside him. Thomas and Leora sprang to mind. He could not imagine the pain of losing someone so young. He shivered at the thought of them disfigured. Some encouragement was necessary. "You must give it time. When I lost my wife, I thought I would never pull myself out of the grief and rage that threatened to consume me."

"What saved you?" Andrew asked.

"God. And, also, nature. I spent a lot of time outdoors, searching. Nature teaches us that nothing is permanent, no matter how much it feels like it is. The changing seasons mean that we change, and so do our lives. Those painful experiences do not define our lives but can help us grow. Delicate buds break through the ground and boldly flower in the spring with renewed life. So can you, Andrew. People can overcome hardship to bloom once more."

"What if I am beyond saving?"

"No one is beyond help," Isaiah said. "It may not feel like it yet, but you've come to the right place."

Andrew cleared his throat. "I can go and get help, but I'm afraid to drive again."

"We can see about getting you a buggy."

Andrew smiled as if he liked the thought.

CHAPTER 9: IMPORTANT DECISIONS

The Lapps returned home just as the first star appeared in the indigo sky. The days were short, so it was just before suppertime. It had been a long and eventful day, but they still had to reckon with Mrs. Lapp. As they walked through the gate, Samuel greeted them while sitting on their porch swing, the same place where he would wait for Rachel during their courtship. Mary turned to her father for direction.

"Go and talk to him. I had better go inside and explain to your *maem*—who is probably pacing the floors—what happened with Dr. Brown."

Mary nodded, then took her seat next to Samuel on the swing. She was giddy to be sitting in Rachel's place. *So, this is what it feels like to have a gentleman caller,* she thought. "Are you okay?" she asked Samuel.

"I'm fine. How is Dr. Brown?"

"He's as well as can be expected. Isaiah took him home, then to the hospital. He's eager to heal, and he hopes that therapy will do the trick. He trusts Isaiah."

"*Danki,* Mary. I don't know what would have happened if it weren't for you and your *daed.*

"And you," Mary reminded him. "You're the one who rescued Dr. Brown."

Samuel was unconvinced. His failures dejected him. "I still feel like this is all my fault. Your *daed* was right. I should have come to him sooner. What if Dr. Brown had hurt himself? Or worse? It was stupid of me to keep him locked up in the cottage." He looked to Mary with big, doe-like eyes. "At least you had the sense and the courage to tell someone. Who knows what would have happened had it been left up to me?"

"You have no reason to be self-deprecating, Sam. It was an impossible situation, and we can be grateful for the way it turned out. Dr. Brown is getting the help he needs, and no one was seriously hurt."

Samuel nodded, then managed a smile. Mary understood him and encouraged him. It was what he needed to stop being his father and grandfather before him.

"How did it go with your *daed*?" Mary asked. "Did you manage to talk to him?"

Samuel sighed and leaned back in the swing. "I don't think my *daed* and I will ever be able to understand one another. He told me that he wants me to be a man of worth and substance and implied that I should be more like him."

Mary reached for Samuel's hand and held it under her own. "That's who you already are. I wish that you would not let him make you feel bad about yourself, Sam."

"You'd think that after all of these years, I'd be used to disappointing him."

"You didn't disappoint me. That's twice now."

Samuel leaned in and whispered, "How do you do that?"

Excited by his undivided attention, Mary asked, "Do what?"

"Make me feel like I'm the tallest man in the world."

"You make it so easy to believe in you."

Samuel's smile brightened the night. Then, there, on the little porch swing, in a perfect moment that Mary had only dreamed of, and with no Thomas to interrupt them this time, Mary Lapp closed her eyes and let Samuel gently kiss her. The two leaned back into the seat and exhaled like they had just enjoyed a Christmas banquet. Mary wondered if any dream she dreamed henceforth would be as sweet as her first kiss. She bid her beau goodnight and fled into the house where she could savor the moment.

Samuel stepped away from the Lapp house, his mind dancing through the day's memories to finally come to rest on Mary. Samuel could not quite explain what had evolved between them, for she had never been his interest, yet a life without Mary now seemed inconceivable. And what a find! She had managed to become the most important person in Samuel's life in a matter of weeks. What astonished him further was how naturally she had come to occupy that space. Mary had just slotted into the hole in his heart like the missing piece of a puzzle.

* * *

Andrew's story had shaken Isaiah. He had lost an adult, but a child? And one so dear? *Life is too short,* he reasoned. He hurried to find Adel.

Leora's mother stood in the kitchen, cleaning up the last of the dishes. She wore a kerchief on her head, her hair braided and laying over her shoulder. She seemed quite at home, and that is where Isaiah wanted to keep her.

"Adel?"

The woman turned and smiled. "You're back! How was it with Levi?"

Isaiah looked confused, having completely forgotten why it was he had left her at home, his mind rehearsing what he had wanted to say. "Oh, yes, well, it went well. I mean, the bishop wasn't home, but it turned out he was already at the King farm, so I went alone, but I ran into Levi first, but then, Andrew was there."

"The man who hit you?"

"Yes. He'd been staying with Samuel ever since the baby was born."

"Leora?"

"Yes. He came to the hospital to visit me, thinking I was still there, and saw us together. He thought that you were my wife. The baby's crying set him off—"

"What is it?"

"He lost a child, a patient, when he was a doctor. His story made me realize—life is too short. I know we haven't known each other that long, but I can't imagine not having you or Leora in my life. My life is incomplete without you. Jo will always have a place in my heart, as I'm sure Daniel will in yours. But we deserve to be happy now. I'm more afraid not to have you than to lose you. Adel, will you be my wife?"

CHAPTER 10: THE LEAP

ary lazed about in bed, something uncommon in an
Amish household, yet much deserved after the events
of the previous day. The cream ceiling grew lighter
as the first rays of sun came through the crack in the curtain.
Having been awake for a little while, she replayed in her mind all
that had happened since winter's start. What she had expected
to be lonesome and dull had turned out to be anything but when
Samuel had come knocking at the door. Why had he come to
her? Why had he chosen to trust her? And how did they come to
the place where they were in love? *Love!* Mary sat up in bed and
gasped. The adventures with Samuel King had overwhelmed her
so much so that she had forgotten which day it was. Mary jumped
out of bed and hurried downstairs to find her mother already in
the kitchen, preparing breakfast.

"*Maem*, what day is it?"

Mrs. Lapp turned around and frowned at her daughter.
"Mary, I am surprised at you," she remarked. "I thought you'd
be dressed and ready to go to the Weavers. Your *daed* is already
dressed and getting the horses."

"So, it's Tuesday?" Mary clarified.

Mrs. Lapp looked disdainful. "Yes, of course, it is! And need
I remind you that Abigael and Sarah will expect all their *newe-*

hockers there early? Goodness, *Dochder*!"

Oh no! I forgot that the Weavers are getting married! "Sorry, *Maem*," Mary mumbled as she hurried back upstairs and opened her cupboard to find her periwinkle blue dress. Mary threw it on and quickly made herself presentable, tucking her unruly curls neatly beneath her *kapp*. She grumbled to herself for being so silly as to forget such an important day. Once ready, she went back downstairs to help finish breakfast.

"Well, don't you look nice," Mrs. Lapp said approvingly. "That dress suits you."

Mary gave her a shy smile. It was unusual for her mother to comment on her appearance. Mary took special pride in her words but then had to be humble lest she sin.

"I think the Weaver sisters chose a particularly pleasant shade of blue," Mrs. Lapp added approvingly.

Mary nodded in agreement. Unlike in English traditions where it was considered a faux pas to wear white, which was reserved for the bride, in Amish communities, the female attendants wore the same shade as the bride on her wedding day. Mary liked this tradition because marriages were as much between the couple as they were a celebration for the whole community.

"You're *daed* is going over to the Weaver house after breakfast to talk to the couples before the ceremony."

Mary nodded. "I will go with him."

Mrs. Lapp nodded as though it went without saying. The Lapps ate their breakfast in comfortable silence, preoccupied in their own thoughts.

"Shall we go?" Bishop Lapp asked as he placed his knife and fork together on his empty plate.

Mary nodded and rose from the table.

"I'll see you both at the Weavers' house in a little while," Mrs. Lapp said.

As Mary and Bishop Lapp made their way along the road toward the Weaver farm, Abigael and Sarah were getting ready for their big day. While Mary had been surprised that the weddings had come so quickly, Abigael and Sarah thought quite the opposite. Both sisters were up long before the sun that morning to make sure they had enough time to get all their chores done.

"I can't believe we're getting married today," Abigael said excitedly.

"I know," Sarah agreed.

"I'm glad we decided to get married on the same day," said Abigael.

Initially, Abigael had not wanted to get married on the same day as Sarah because she wanted it to feel special. After all, they did everything together. Sarah had eventually won her over, saying that it was the last thing they would do together before moving into separate homes and living separate lives. "After all," she had said, "it's not like we can deliver a baby together! I'd like to have this one final experience with you."

Abigael appreciated Sarah's sentiment. In the end, she had agreed. Now, though, they were in each other's way.

"Help me, please?"

Sarah nodded and reached over to help Abigael tie her white apron strings over her blue dress. Their mother knocked at the door.

"Bishop Lapp is here," Mrs. Weaver said.

"We'll be right there," the twins chimed.

"This is it," Abigael said as she grabbed hold of Sarah's hands and squeezed them tightly. "I love you, *Schweschder*, and I hope that *Gott* brings you and Jacob a lifetime of happiness and a house filled with beautiful children."

Sarah looked at her twin, teary-eyed.

"Don't cry," Abigael warned. "You'll make your face all blotchy."

Despite herself, Sarah chuckled. "I love you, Abi. You look radiant."

Abigael smiled and wrapped her arms around her sister. "Let's do this." Abigael grabbed Sarah's hand and led her out of the door, down the stairs, and toward the rest of their lives.

Mary stood by her father when the twins emerged from their room.

"Mary!" Sarah said. "We're getting married today!"

Mary laughed. "I know. I'm so happy for you both." Mary looked at Abigael as she spoke. She knew that they had not always seen eye to eye, but they had been friends since they were little girls playing hopscotch on the playground.

"I'd like to speak to you both before the ceremony begins, so that you know what to expect today," Bishop Lapp explained.

Sarah and Abigael nodded.

"Shall we go into the sitting room?" Bishop Lapp suggested.

Sarah led the way, and Bishop Lapp followed. Before Abigael went after them, she leaned toward Mary. "It'll be your turn next."

Mary looked surprised.

"Don't think you can fool me, Mary Lapp," Abigael said. "I saw you and Samuel King together in the garden, and if that isn't love, then I'm a hippopotamus."

Mary laughed when she felt her cheeks flush, but Abigael had hurried away into the sitting room before she could respond.

Mary headed toward the kitchen to ask Mrs. Weaver if she needed help with the preparations.

❋ ❋ ❋

The buggies pulled onto the Weaver homestead, and the guests' murmurs grew to a ruckus as more arrived. The men outside could be heard chattering, occasionally barking out directives as to where to park. Just like at church, the women and children entered the home while the men gathered outdoors to talk weather and crops. The youth formed their own circles.

"Mary," a soft voice said.

Mary turned around and saw the kind face of Hannah King. She, too, was dressed in an attendant dress, and the color matched her soft blue eyes perfectly.

"Hannah," Mary said. "It's so lovely to see you."

Mary could not help but notice that Hannah looked tired, and she wondered if all was well in the King household since the Dr. Brown incident.

"I'm so sorry I'm late," she said. "Did Abigael or Sarah say anything?"

"Don't worry," Mary said. "They didn't notice."

Hannah looked relieved.

"Is Samuel here?" Mary asked, looking around.

She saw Mr. and Mrs. King talking to the Troyers, but there was no sign of Samuel.

Hannah shook her head.

"No, but he asked me to give you this."

Hannah handed Mary a carefully folded sheet of paper. Mary was about to open it when her father cleared his throat, and the whole room fell silent. Mary palmed the note, smiled at Hannah, and found her place with the other *newehockers.*

"Let us begin," Bishop Lapp said. "Today is a very happy day indeed, for *Gott* has brought together these two couples in these blessed unions."

Mary watched Abigael, Amos, Sarah, and Jacob, all smiling, unable to take their eyes off one another. For so many months, Mary had witnessed her friends exchange these exact expressions to each other but had not been able to relate. Now, however, she knew exactly what it was like to be in love.

As with Amish custom, the ceremony went on until midday. Halfway through, when the congregation was cheerfully singing hymns, Bishop Lapp called Abigael and Amos away to counsel them. When they returned, he asked Sarah and Jacob to do the same. During their counsel, Mary stole away to the bathroom, unable to contain her curiosity any longer. She had to know what Samuel had written to her. Tucked safely behind the wooden door, Mary unfolded the paper.

Mary,

I am sorry not to see you at the weddings today. I've gone back to the city for now. I need to close this chapter of my life before I can open a new one. I hope you can understand. Things are more complicated than ever with my daed, *and I need some time to think about what I want.*

I am not sure when I'll be back, but I hope soon. I'll be in touch.
Samuel

Mary stared at the note in her hands, and she felt her stomach sink. She was unsure what Samuel's words meant for them. The kiss on the porch had meant everything to her, but perhaps it had not meant as much to Samuel. Suddenly, Mary heard the chorus of voices singing, so she quickly headed back to join the rest of the congregation, dizzy from this latest revelation.

At midday, the ceremony ended, and the young couples were officially married. It was a happy occasion, though Mary plastered a disingenuous smile on her face. Samuel's words haunted her, *I am not sure when I'll be back, but I hope soon.* Mary was in everyone's way, however, because the space had to be prepared for the banquet. Men moved the chairs and set up the tables while the women prepared the food and served.

Abigael, Amos, Sarah, and Jacob were seated at the corner table, and Hannah, Mary, and Aaron were sitting nearest them. The tables were all decorated with fresh, white, linen clothes and stalks of celery in vases down the center of the table. Some had come from their garden.

As Mary looked across at the rows of familiar faces, she saw Rachel and Noah with Jo between them. Rachel caught her eye and waved, and Mary waved back. She wondered if her sister might see something was wrong, but Rachel was distracted by something little Thomas said and looked away. Seated next to them were Isaiah and Adel. They were holding hands and staring into each other's eyes as if there was no one else in the room. Everywhere Mary looked, she saw love, happiness, and contentment, and yet she felt so empty.

"Are you okay?" Aaron asked. "You've hardly eaten two bites of your food."

Mary looked up from her plate. "I'm just not hungry. Too much excitement."

Aaron nodded. "It's strange to think how young we all were just earlier this year. We were all still at school, starting a garden with no idea what the future had in store. Now half of us are married—"

"And one of us is leaving," Mary interjected.

"*Ya*," Aaron agreed. "And what about you, Mary Lapp?"

"What about me?" Mary asked.

"You can't tell me that you don't have grand designs for the future."

Mary felt tears in her eyes, so she got up from the table. "Excuse me."

"Mary!"

But Mary was already hurrying across the room and out of the front door. She went wherever her feet carried her. She stopped before standing at the little garden gate. She pushed it open and went inside. She heard footsteps behind her.

"I just need a few minutes, Aaron," Mary said softly.

"It's not Aaron," a voice replied.

Mary whirled around to see Samuel. "What are you doing here?" Her tone was aggressive, and it surprised her. She had not realized how angry she was.

"You're angry. Did you get my note?"

Mary nodded. "You left, Samuel. After everything I said to you last night and everything that happened between us, you left without an indication of when or if you were ever coming back. Do you know how that made me feel?"

"I know," he said. "I'm sorry, Mary. I didn't mean to hurt you. It's the last thing in the world I would ever want to do."

"Then why did you?"

"Because I'm an idiot," Samuel admitted. "I thought that maybe you'd be better off without my drama, and so I ran, like a coward."

Mary wiped her tears. "Why did you come back?"

Samuel smiled. "I was sitting on the train and watching the blurred landscape pass outside of the window, and I think that I must have fallen asleep because suddenly I heard your voice. It was as if you were sitting right next to me whispering in my ear."

Despite herself, Mary looked at him curiously. "What did I say?"

"You said, 'Don't be an idiot, Samuel. Don't give up on the life you want because you're afraid that you don't deserve it. Be the man of substance and worth I know you are.'"

Samuel's words took her breath away, but she was not yet calm. "Well, dream-Mary sounds like she knows what she's talking about," Mary said, arms crossed.

Samuel smiled.

"And so that's why you came back?" Mary pressed.

"As soon as the train arrived in the city, I bought a ticket to come right back home," Samuel explained.

Mary nodded.

"Will you forgive me, Mary?"

"You scared me, Samuel."

"I can tell."

"How can I trust that you won't do it again?" Mary asked.

"Because I hate seeing you scared. I want to be by your side so you don't ever have to be scared again. Leap with me, Mary. I can't promise that there won't be times when I'm insecure and question myself, but I can promise you from this moment on that I will never question *us*. That train ride back was the longest journey of my life, and it made me realize that I never want to take another step without you by my side."

Samuel's eyes eased Mary's fears. The letter had burst open

her insecurities. She was afraid of never being loved. It was clear that neither she nor Samuel was perfect. Their pasts had left them both riddled with insecurities. With *Gott's* guidance, however, they would be able to carve a path together.

"I love you, Samuel King," Mary said. "I'll leap with you as long as you never leave me again."

Mary's bold proclamation took Samuel by surprise, but he did not hesitate or falter. "We may have known each other our whole lives, and I've never thought of you as anything other than Rachel's little *schweschder*, but you're the one for me, Mary Lapp. *Gott's* ways are mysterious, but His plans and timing are perfect. Who knew that an *Englisch* doctor would be the one to bring us together? We couldn't have orchestrated this story even if we had tried. I'll never leave you, and I'll love you forever and always."

Mary smiled up at Samuel, but suddenly she faltered.

"What is it?" Samuel asked.

"What are our parents going to say?"

Samuel grimaced. "Maybe let's wait until tomorrow to tell them?"

"*Gut* idea," Mary agreed. Then she reached up on her toes and kissed Samuel's smiling mouth. "We'd better get back." She grabbed Samuel's hand and led him through the garden, the first of many steps that they would take together, hand-in-hand and side-by-side.

Mary and Samuel returned to the celebrations. They had decided not to say anything to anyone just yet. After all, it was new to them, and there were others to celebrate. It was only right to keep the Weaver wedding day about the Weavers.

"May I walk you home?" Samuel asked when the celebrations ended.

"*Ya, danki*," Mary agreed.

They took a long, slow walk back along the road, enjoying the peace and quiet.

"Samuel?"

"*Ya?*"

"I love you, but I don't want you to give up your dreams for me."

Samuel frowned.

"If you stay here, then that means you are committing to a life of farming. Is that really what you want?"

Samuel sighed. "The truth is, Mary, that until today, I had not decided what I wanted. But now I know that I want a life with you, and I want to give you a home and children." Mary's silence compelled him to fill the silence. "What I really want to know is more about the Bible. I can understand the *Englisch* one. We can't tell our elders—especially your *daed*—or I'll be shunned! I know that I want to walk hand-in-hand with you while our children pick corn off the cob. They will play with the lambs in the fields. I want to create a life for us in the country where the sun warms our faces and where we grow old sitting on the front porch watching the change of seasons."

Mary listened to Samuel's words, and they painted the most vivid picture in her mind. She saw their beautiful children with chestnut curls laughing as they ran across the garden on a warm summer's afternoon. She saw them picking daisies in the spring and jumping in the piles of autumn leaves. She saw their flushed cheeks as they built snowmen with pebble eyes and carrot stick noses. It was the most beautiful picture that Mary had ever imagined, and she wanted it all so badly that it made her heart ache.

"I want that too," Mary whispered. "I want you to be by my

side when every spring flower blooms and when the last snow-flake falls at every winter's end."

Samuel grabbed Mary's hand and squeezed it tightly. They did not speak the rest of the way home, for the moment had said it all.

EPILOGUE

Following the Weavers' wedding, the community celebrated three more weddings before the Christmas season was upon them. After that, everyone found themselves preoccupied with their Christmas meal plans and prepared for family's and friends' arrival. The news of their union did not surprise Bishop and Mrs. Lapp, who were happy for Mary and Samuel. Levi King had not taken the news as well as Mary's parents, but that was to be expected. The young couple was relieved that he kept his mouth shut, considering it progress.

Mary had been concerned about how Rachel would react to the news, but she was pleasantly surprised. Rachel had been more than pleased that Mary had finally found someone to love, and she thought that Samuel was the ideal choice.

"I am so happy for you, Mary," Rachel said. Her sister hugged her tightly, and Mary cried in relief.

"I was so nervous to tell you," Mary confessed.

"Well, I am glad you did," Rachel said. "You and Samuel together just make everything perfect. I can't believe I didn't see it before. You are two of my favorite people, and it makes absolute sense that you should be together."

It was strange to Mary how everything just fell into place

that winter. Shortly before Christmas, Andrew was released from the hospital, and Isaiah invited him to stay at the Fisher farm for Christmas, then hired him as a farm hand. Andrew had shown interest in joining the Amish, so Isaiah had approached his bishop for permission for Dr. Brown to remain in the community. Being in the heart of the community, surrounded by nature, would be the ideal place for him to heal.

"How is he?" Bishop Lapp asked.

"He's better," Isaiah said. "He's still shaken. I hope his time with us will help."

Bishop Lapp nodded.

"That kind of trauma is hard to erase."

"I just hope that, with the right environment and people around him, he might have a fighting chance," Isaiah confessed.

Bishop Lapp nodded and looked at Isaiah with admiration. He was by far one of the most kindhearted people he had ever come across. "Well, if there is one place that he will feel loved and accepted, it is the Fisher house."

Andrew Brown's friend was, likewise, on the mend. Samuel returned to work at the King Farm, at his father's request. While it was an adjustment, it was a little easier with each passing day. Samuel and Levi found a rhythm, albeit a quiet one. Samuel found conversations with his father stilted and uneasy, so they worked in silence. Still, that was a good thing, since Levi kept any sour opinions to himself. Even the way he looked at his son was now void of contempt, in its place a mild appreciation. This was something neither could have predicted.

"You know, it's strange," Samuel remarked.

"What is?" Mary asked.

She was seated next to Samuel on the buggy. It was late

January, and they were driving through town in the afternoon. The streets were empty except for some children having a snowball fight on the roadside near where Mary's market once stood.

"Do you remember a few months ago when you told me that one day my *daed* and I would find something in each other that we'd recognize, and after that, things wouldn't be as hard?"

Mary nodded. "I'm surprised you remember that," she teased.

"I never forget the things you say to me. You were right. These last few weeks working with my *daed* on the farm, we've developed an unspoken respect for one another. It's almost impossible to explain, but I can feel it between us."

The news made Mary happy. She smiled, and when she did, Samuel's spirits lifted.

"We are a long way from actually talking about anything without arguing, but I really think that the land is giving us a chance to heal. I never believed my *daed* had much of a heart, but when we are out there on the farm, I see it."

"I'm so happy for you, Sam."

Mary knew that it might take a long time for Samuel and Levi to heal their relationship, but she believed that it was possible, and as Samuel's fiancée, she wanted to do whatever she could to help them.

At the end of February, Mary and Samuel received an invitation for Saturday lunch at the Fisher farm. There was no reason given, and so they went along wondering what the occasion might be. Mary stood on her porch, watching the snowflakes fall softly to the ground.

"I reckon this will be the last snowfall of the year," Samuel said.

Mary reached out a hand to catch some of the flakes in her palm. No sooner had they landed on her warm skin than they melted into tiny droplets of water. She sighed.

"You cannot tell me you aren't looking forward to spring," Samuel teased. "You've been talking about winter's end for weeks."

"I know," Mary said. "But now that winter is truly over, I feel sad."

Samuel chuckled. Mary always felt this way at the end of every season. There was something tragic and beautiful about each change. She loved spring and she was excited for what lay ahead in the days to come, but she was also sad to say goodbye to the best winter she had ever known.

"Are you ready to go?" Samuel asked. "If I remember, Rachel was never one for tardiness."

Mary nodded. "You're right. Let's go."

The soft snow had stopped falling by the time they arrived at the Fisher house. Thomas was waiting for them at the gate.

"Hello," he called.

"Hello," Mary replied. "What are you doing out here?"

"I am waiting to escort you inside," Thomas said formally.

Samuel raised his eyebrow and Mary smiled. "Well, isn't that nice," she said.

"This way, if you please," said Thomas. Mary and Samuel followed the little boy inside, trying not to laugh. Rachel was inside to greet them.

"I see you've met our new butler?" Rachel said.

"*Ya*," Mary said. "And I must say it's a vast improvement from my last visit."

Rachel chuckled. "*Willkumm*. It's *gut* to see you both."

"So, what's the occasion?" Mary asked.

Rachel smiled. "You'll find out soon enough. Come, everyone is already in the dining room."

Thomas suddenly cleared his throat.

"Oh, sorry," Rachel said. "Lead the way."

The trio followed Thomas through the house toward the chatter and laughter. The whole Fisher family was there along with Mrs. Yoder, Sarah and Jacob, Andrew Brown, Adel, and Hannah. Hanging across the window was a handmade banner with the word "CONGRATULATIONS!" printed across it.

"Sit down," Rachel insisted.

Mary and Samuel sat down in the two empty chairs. Mary caught Abigael's eye. *It's you, isn't it?* she mouthed.

Abigael stuck her tongue out at Mary, and both girls giggled childishly.

"Well, now that everyone is here, we would like to announce that Amos and Abigael are expecting!" Isaiah said. He paused for the gasps and cheers, then added, "I think we should eat."

Abigael was surrounded by the other girls who couldn't believe her luck. The men nodded to Amos, then picked up the plates and passed them to one another, making sure that everyone had a spoonful of everything. While people served and chatted merrily, Rachel leaned across to Mary. "I have something to tell you," she whispered, "but it's not public knowledge yet."

"What is it?" Mary asked.

"Jo is going to be a big sister."

Mary shrieked and threw her arms around Rachel, causing the rest of the table to stop talking and look at them.

"Sorry," Rachel commented. "Mary sometimes gets overly

excited about cinnamon sweet potatoes. Has done so since we were kids."

Mary grinned sheepishly as she caught Noah's eye, and he winked.

"This is so perfect," Mary whispered. "Do you know when?"

"November, we think."

"That's just in time for our wedding," Mary said.

It was Rachel's turn to shriek with excitement, drawing eyes on her once more.

"Those sweet potatoes are quite a crowd-pleaser," Mary exclaimed.

The rest took their seats, but Aaron stopped Hannah before she joined the women's table. "Did you ever tell your brother what I did?" Aaron asked.

"No. Why should I?" asked Hannah.

"Hasn't he ever wondered how the *Englischer* could have stayed warm when all he brought him was food?"

"I suppose he hasn't."

"I'm glad I did it, you know."

Hannah was shy. "Me too."

"Oh, yeah? Why?" Aaron knew exactly what she was thinking, but it sounded sweeter and softer coming from her mouth.

"Because." Hannah pursed her lips and looked up, innocently, then looked back at her boyfriend. "I got you." She did a little jig with her shoulders.

"Oh! You look precious!" Then, Aaron got serious. "I'm glad that I decided to stay. That was a lot of wood to chop and stack! But you convinced me that this is the life I want and that I want it with you."

Hannah smiled at her food, then went to join the other

ladies. Aaron could not take his eyes off her. It was only when all were seated that he felt self-conscious and dared to look away. He missed Hannah's return gaze, but Mary caught it and smiled.

* * *

"How about we take a walk in the garden before I take you home?" Samuel suggested.

Mary smiled. They walked to the garden. The snowflakes from earlier had disappeared since the sun had turned its head from behind the clouds to beam at the small plot in which Mary had grown over the past year. Mary led Samuel to the dogwood tree, then gasped.

"What is it?" Samuel asked.

"Look up!"

Samuel did as he was told. The branches of the dogwood were covered in little swollen buds, about to burst.

Samuel took Mary's hand as they wandered around the garden. Each path they took and every corner they turned was brimming with sprouts. The old Mary of the garden was gone. Instead, in the same place, would bud her burgeoning romance.

"Every end is just the beginning," said Mary.

Thank you, readers!

Thank you for reading this book. It is important to me to share my stories with you and that you enjoy them. May I ask of you a favor? If you enjoyed this book, will you please take a moment to leave a review on Amazon and/or Goodreads? Thank you for your support!

Also, each week, I send my readers updates about my life as well as information about my new releases, freebies, promos, and book recommendations. If you're interested in receiving my weekly newsletter, please go to newsletter.sylviaprice.com, and it will ask you for your email. As a thank-you, you will receive a FREE exclusive short story that isn't available for purchase!

Blessings,
Sylvia

BOOKS IN THIS SERIES

Amish Love Through the Seasons
Featuring many of the beloved characters from Sylvia Price's bestseller, The Christmas Arrival, as well as a new cast of characters, Amish Love Through the Seasons centers around a group of teenagers as they find friendship, love, and hope in the midst of trials.

Tragedy strikes a small Amish community outside of Erie, Pennsylvania when Isaiah Fisher, a widower and father of three, is involved in a serious accident. When his family is left scrambling to pick up the pieces, the community unites to help the single father, but the hospital bills keep piling up. How will the family manage?

Mary Lapp, a youth in the community, decides to take up Isaiah's cause. She enlists the help of other teenagers to plant a garden and sell the produce. While tending to the garden, new relationships develop, but old ones are torn apart. With tensions mounting, will the youth get past their disagreements in order to reconcile and produce fruit? Will they each find love? Join them on their adventure through the seasons!

Seeds Of Spring Love (Book 1)

Sprouts Of Summer Love (Book 2)

Fruits Of Fall Love (Book 3)

Waiting For Winter Love (Book 4)

BOOKS BY THIS AUTHOR

The Crystal Crescent Inn (Sambro Lighthouse Book 1)

The Sambro Lighthouse Series, set on Canada's picturesque Crystal Crescent Beach, is a feel-good read perfect for fans of second chances with a bit of history and mystery all rolled into one.

Liz Beckett is grief-stricken when her beloved husband of thirty-five years dies after a long battle with cancer. Her daughter and best friend insist she needs a project to keep her occupied. Liz decides to share the beauty of Crystal Crescent Beach with those who visit the beautiful east coast of Nova Scotia and prepares to embark on the adventure of her life. She moves into the converted art studio at the bottom of her garden and turns the old family home into The Crystal Crescent Inn.

One of her first visitors is famous archeologist, Merc MacGill, and he's not there to admire the view. The handsome bachelor believes there's an undiscovered eighteenth-century farmstead hidden inside the creeks and coves of Crystal Crescent, and Liz wants to help him find it.

But it's not all smooth sailing at the inn that overlooks the historic Sambro Lighthouse. No one has realized it yet, but the lives of everyone in Liz's family are intertwined with those first settlers who landed in Nova Scotia over two hundred and fifty years ago. Will they be able to unravel the mystery? Will the lives of

Liz's two children be changed forever if they discover the link between the lighthouse and their old home?

Take a trip to Crystal Crescent Beach and join Liz, her family, and guests as they navigate the storms and calm waters of life and love under the watchful eye of the lighthouse and its secret.

The Christmas Arrival

Rachel Lapp is a young Amish woman who is the daughter of the community's bishop. She is in the midst of planning the annual Christmas Nativity play when newcomer Noah Miller arrives in town to spend Christmas with his cousins. Encouraged by her father to welcome the new arrival, Rachel asks Noah to be a part of the Nativity.

Despite Rachel's engagement to Samuel King, a local farmer, she finds herself irrevocably drawn to Noah and his carefree spirit. Reserved and slightly shy, Noah is hesitant to get involved in the play, but an unlikely friendship begins to develop between Rachel and Noah, bringing with it unexpected problems, including a seemingly harmless prank with life-threatening consequences that require a Christmas miracle.

Will Rachel honor her commitment to Samuel, or will Noah win her affections?

Join these characters on what is sure to be a heartwarming holiday adventure! Instead of waiting for each part to be released, enjoy the entire Christmas Arrival series in this exclusive collection!

Jonah's Redemption (Book 1)

Available for FREE on Amazon

Jonah has lost his community, and he's struggling to get by in the English world. He yearns for his Amish roots, but his past mistakes keep him from returning home.

Mary Lou is recovering from a medical scare. Her journey has impressed upon her how precious life is, so she decides to go on rumspringa to see the world.

While in the city, Mary Lou meets Jonah. Unable to understand his foul attitude, especially towards her, she makes every effort to share her faith with him. As she helps him heal from his past, an attraction develops.

Will Jonah's heart soften towards Mary Lou? What will God do with these two broken people?

Jonah's Redemption Boxed Set (Books 2-5, Epilogue, And Companion Story)

If you loved Jonah's Redemption: Book 1 (available for free on Amazon), grab the rest of the series in this special boxed set featuring Books 2-5, plus a bonus epilogue and companion story, "Jonah's Reminiscence."

Mary Lou's fiancé leaves her as soon as tragedy strikes. Unwilling to resent him, she chooses, instead, to find him. Her misfortunes pile up in her quest to return Jonah to the Amish faith, but she is undeterred, for God has given her a mission.

Will Mary Lou's faith be enough to help them get through the countless obstacles that are thrown their way? Do Jonah and Mary Lou have a chance at happiness?

Join Jonah and Mary Lou as they wrestle with love, a life worth living, and their unique faith in Christ. Enjoy the conclusion of

Jonah's Redemption in this exclusive boxed set, with a bonus epilogue and companion story!

Songbird Cottage Beginnings (Pleasant Bay Prequel)

Available for FREE on Amazon

Set on Canada's picturesque Cape Breton Island, this book is perfect for those who enjoy new beginnings and countryside landscapes.

Sam MacAuley and his wife Annalize are total opposites. When Sam wants to leave city life in Halifax to get a plot of land on Cape Breton Island, where he grew up, his wife wants nothing to do with his plans and opts to move herself and their three boys back to her home country of South Africa.

As Sam settles into a new life on his own, his friend Lachlan encourages him to get back into the dating scene. Although he meets plenty of women, he longs to find the one with whom he wants to share the rest of his life. Will Sam ever meet "the one"?

Get to know Sam and discover the origins of the Songbird Cottage.

This is the prequel to the rest of the Pleasant Bay series.

The Songbird Cottage (Pleasant Bay Book 1)

A feel-good read about family loyalties and second chances set on Canada's picturesque Cape Breton Island, this book is perfect for those who enjoy sweet romances and countryside landscapes.

Emma Copeland and her daughters, Claire and Isabelle, spend

their summers at Songbird Cottage in Pleasant Bay, Nova Scotia. While there, Emma enjoys the company of her ruggedly handsome neighbor, Sam MacAuley, but when something happens between them, she vows never to return to Songbird Cottage.

When Emma turns fifty, she rushes into a marriage with smooth-talking Andrew Schönfeld, but when he suddenly dies, Emma loses everything.

With her life in shambles, and with nowhere else to stay, Emma returns to Songbird Cottage. Despite leaving without an explanation eighteen years ago, Sam is quick to Emma's aid when she arrives on Cape Breton.

As the beauty and peacefulness of Pleasant Bay begin to heal Emma, she gets some shocking news, and she discovers that she's unwelcomed at Songbird Cottage. Will she be able to piece her life back together and get another chance at happiness?

Join Emma as she begins a new life on Cape Breton Island, and get to know her family and the friendly locals.

The Songbird Cottage Boxed Set (Pleasant Bay Complete Series Collection)

If you loved Songbird Cottage Beginnings (available for free on Amazon), grab the rest of the series in this special boxed set.

Amazon bestselling author Sylvia Price's Pleasant Bay series is a feel-good read about family loyalties and second chances set on Canada's picturesque Cape Breton Island. This series is perfect for those who enjoy sweet romances and countryside landscapes. Enjoy all these sweet romance books in one collection for the first time!

Emma Copeland and her daughters, Claire and Isabelle, spend their summers at Songbird Cottage in Pleasant Bay, Nova Scotia. While there, Emma enjoys the company of her ruggedly handsome neighbor, Sam MacAuley, but when something happens between them, she vows never to return to Songbird Cottage.

When Emma turns fifty, she rushes into a marriage with smooth-talking Andrew Schönfeld, but when he suddenly dies, Emma loses everything.

With her life in shambles, and with nowhere else to stay, Emma returns to Songbird Cottage. Despite leaving without an explanation eighteen years ago, Sam is quick to Emma's aid when she arrives on Cape Breton.

As the beauty and peacefulness of Pleasant Bay begin to heal Emma, she gets some shocking news, and she discovers that she's unwelcomed at Songbird Cottage. Will she be able to piece her life back together and get another chance at happiness?

Join Emma Copeland and her daughters, Claire and Isabelle, get to know their family and neighbors, and explore the magic of Songbird Cottage.

Included in this set are all the popular titles:

The Songbird Cottage
Return to Songbird Cottage
Escape to Songbird Cottage
Secrets of Songbird Cottage
Seasons at Songbird Cottage

ABOUT THE AUTHOR

Now an Amazon bestselling author, Sylvia Price is an author of Amish and contemporary romance and women's fiction. She especially loves writing uplifting stories about second chances!

Sylvia was inspired to write about the Amish as a result of the enduring legacy of Mennonite missionaries in her life. While living with them for three weeks, they got her a library card and encouraged her to start reading to cope with the loss of television and radio, giving Sylvia a new-found appreciation for books.

Although raised in the cosmopolitan city of Montréal, Sylvia spent her adolescent and young adult years in Nova Scotia, and the beautiful countryside landscapes and ocean views serve as the backdrop to her contemporary novels.

After meeting and falling in love with an American while living abroad, Sylvia now resides in the US. She spends her days writing, hoping to inspire the next generation to read more stories. When she's not writing, Sylvia stays busy making sure her three young children are alive and well-fed.

Subscribe to Sylvia's newsletter at newsletter.sylviaprice.com to stay in the loop about new releases, freebies, promos, and more. As a thank-you, you will receive a FREE exclusive short story that isn't available for purchase!

Learn more about Sylvia at amazon.com/author/sylviaprice and goodreads.com/author/show/1134593.Sylvia_Price.

Follow Sylvia on Facebook at facebook.com/sylviapriceauthor for updates.

Join Sylvia's Advanced Reader Copies (ARC) team at arcteam.sylviaprice.com to get her books for free before they are released in exchange for honest reviews.